THAT CE

"I had a gr̲e̲a̲t̲ ̲t̲i̲m̲e̲," Woody said.

"So did I," I murmured.

Actually it wouldn't have been half bad if it hadn't been for those Honeybees sitting right behind us in the theater, watching my every move.

Then Woody put his arm around me, and I knew the big moment had arrived. *Forgive me, Brandon,* I thought. *I'm only doing this for you.* I closed my eyes and raised my lips to meet Woody's kiss. To my surprise, it was kind of nice—soft and warm and comfortable, like my favorite old sweatshirt. I was a little disappointed when Woody raised his head and drew back.

You're doing this for Brandon, I reminded myself sternly. *You're not supposed to enjoy it!*

Bantam titles in the Sweet Dreams series. Ask your bookseller for titles you have missed:

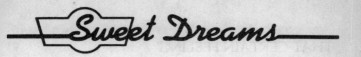

THAT CERTAIN
FEELING

Sheri Cobb South

DORSET COUNTY BANTAM BOOKS
NEW YORK · TORONTO · LONDON · SYDNEY · AUCKLAND

THAT CERTAIN FEELING

A BANTAM BOOK 0 553 29354 0

First publication in Great Britain

PRINTING HISTORY
Bantam edition published 1992

Cover photo by Pat Hill

Bantam Books are published by Transworld Publishers Ltd.,
61–63 Uxbridge Road, Ealing, London W5 5SA,
in Australia by Transworld Publishers (Australia) Pty. Ltd.,
15–23 Helles Avenue, Moorebank, NSW 2170, and in New
Zealand by Transworld Publishers (N.Z.) Ltd.,
3 William Pickering Drive, Albany, Auckland.

Made and printed in Great Britain by
BPCC Hazells Ltd
Member of BPCC Ltd

THAT CERTAIN FEELING

Chapter One

When I first saw the envelope in my locker, I thought it must belong to Melissa, my best friend and locker mate. But a closer look revealed my own name, printed in bold black calligraphy on shiny gold-colored stationery: Miss Penelope Ann Collier.

"Aren't we formal?" I remarked to nobody in particular. "Nobody ever calls me Penelope."

My curiosity certainly was aroused. I was almost positive that the envelope hadn't been there when I'd stopped by my locker an hour earlier. I tore open the flap, pulled out the card, and read it. Unable to trust my eyes, I read it again, and then again, and I was still staring at it in disbelief when Melissa came up behind me.

"Hey, Pen," she said. "What's up?"

How could she sound so flippant on the most important day of my life?

"Melissa, you wouldn't do something like this as a joke, would you?" I asked, suddenly suspicious.

"Something like what?"

Melissa shoved her math book into our overflowing locker and snatched the card out of my hand. She scanned it quickly, then stared at me with a look of utter amazement.

"Penny! You've been invited to join the Honeybees!"

"Then you *didn't* do this as a joke?"

"Would I joke about a thing like this? The Honeybees are the most popular girls in school! Why did they pick *you*?"

Melissa's assessment wasn't exactly complimentary, but I wasn't offended; I'd been wondering the same thing myself.

"I don't know," I confessed. "Last spring I typed Julie Ferguson's term paper for her, and she's on the membership committee. That's not the sort of thing that gets you an invitation, though. Maybe they made a mistake. Maybe this invitation was meant for somebody else."

"Somebody else who just happened to be named Penelope Collier? I think not! Besides," she added loyally, "why *shouldn't* the Honeybees ask you to join?"

"Oh, Melissa, I can't believe it! This is the most exciting thing that's ever happened to me!"

"Maybe you can help me get in next year. Won't it be great? You'll get to wear one of those yellow satin jackets, and hang around with the jocks, and—"

"—and meet Brandon Phillips," I said reverently.

"Brandon Phillips?" Melissa echoed, staring at me as if she'd never seen me before. "You never told me you were interested in Brandon Phillips."

I shrugged. "There didn't seem to be much point in it. After all, he's only the best-looking guy at Pressler High, besides being a senior and the captain of the basketball team. And everybody knows that the Pressler Yellow Jackets only date Honeybees. It's sort of an unwritten law."

Melissa studied the invitation thoughtfully. "But if you're a Honeybee—"

"Not *if*," I corrected her. *"When."*

"Don't be so sure, Penny," Melissa cautioned. "You'll have to go through initiation first, you know. I've heard it can be pretty tough."

"I'll make it," I said resolutely. "I don't care what it takes, I'll make it!"

The rest of the afternoon was a struggle. I knew it wouldn't be cool to run around telling everybody I'd been invited to join the Honeybees, but it was hard not to. After all, things like this didn't happen every day—at least not to me. By the time the bell rang, I just had to tell somebody, so instead of going home, I headed straight for my parents' store.

"Mom! Dad!" I called as I entered.

The bell overhead jangled as I flung open the door, but there was no response from either of my parents. The store seemed to be empty. At three o'clock in the afternoon? That was strange. Collier's Office Supply stayed open till six, and there were usually plenty of customers.

Surely my parents must have left a note. I went behind the counter to look and nearly tripped over a pair of long legs. There on the floor sat a sandy-haired boy eating a sandwich. He was drinking a canned soft drink, too—or at least he had been until I accidentally kicked it over.

"Oh, Woody!" I exclaimed, recognizing Mom and Dad's part-time stock boy. "I'm sorry!"

"It's okay. I was almost done with it anyway." He got up from the floor and moved a stack of schoolbooks away from the puddle of cola spreading across the linoleum. "Hang on a second, and I'll get a mop."

He disappeared into the stockroom through a door marked Employees Only and soon reappeared, carrying a ratty-looking mop. While he went to work cleaning up the spill, I remembered the reason for my visit.

"Woody, where are Mom and Dad?" I asked.

"They've gone to see the contractor about the plans for remodeling the store. They left as soon as I got here, but that wasn't very long ago. It may be a while before they get back."

"Wouldn't you just know it? I've got fantastic news, and nobody to tell it to!"

Woody gave me a funny little smile. "I've got ears, you know."

He did. He also had blue eyes and straight sandy hair that kept flopping into his eyes. He wasn't bad-looking, really. Woody Williams had worked for Mom and Dad since June, but I'd hardly exchanged more than half a dozen words with him in the five months that had passed since then. He'd always seemed sort of bashful to me, maybe even inarticulate. Still, he was human, and I just knew I would explode if I didn't tell somebody my news.

"I've been invited to join the Honeybees!" I announced.

"Honeybees, huh? Sounds painful," Woody remarked, taking another bite of his sandwich. "They sting, you know. I'd pass if I were you."

I laughed. "Not that kind of honeybee! It's a sorority at Pressler. It's *very* exclusive— only the most popular girls get in. I'm still trying to figure out why they picked me."

"So what does a Honeybee do?" Woody asked.

Funny, I'd never really given this much thought.

6

"Well, they take on a couple of projects for charity every year, but mostly they just wear these great-looking gold satin baseball jackets and date the Pressler High jocks," I said finally. Woody had resumed his place on the floor, and for the first time I noticed the blue notebook propped open on his knee. "But I'm interrupting you!"

"No, you're not. I'm interested. Really."

"Are you studying for a big test?"

"You could say that," Woody said with a grin. "It's my playbook for basketball. We've got a new coach, and his system is pretty complicated. I'm a junior at Grayson. This is my first year to play on the varsity."

"I didn't know you played basketball."

" 'Played' might be the right word for it. Last year I started at forward on the jayvee team, but this year I'll probably spend most of my time on the bench."

"Oh, I'm sure you'll—" Woody was forgotten as the bell over the front door jangled, announcing Mom's arrival. "Mom!" I shouted. "Great news!"

I told her the whole story, from my discovery of the envelope in my locker to what an honor it was to be invited to join the Honeybees. Then I left the store and drove home to call everybody I knew and tell them all about it. After all, there was a time to be cool and a time to celebrate, and this was definitely the latter. I was practically a Honeybee, and Brandon Phillips was almost within my reach. Life was wonderful!

Chapter Two

What a day! Only the first day of initiations, and already I was beginning to wonder if this Honeybee thing was all it had been cracked up to be. It was bad enough that I had to get up thirty minutes early in order to chauffeur Honeybee president Sonya Wilcox to school. But Sonya wasn't ready on time, and I was ten minutes late in getting to homeroom. I was too late to buy a lunch ticket—not that I would have had time to eat anyway. The pledges had to sit with the Honeybee officers in the cafeteria and serve them like waitresses, leaving us no time to eat our own lunches. Now it was two o'clock, and I hadn't had a bite since breakfast. I was tired and hungry and . . .

The sound of a whistle in the hall behind me interrupted my thoughts.

"Air raid! Penny Collier! Front and center!"

I turned and saw Fawn Bailey, one of the senior Honeybees, coming in my direction. It could only mean one thing.

"Yes, Fawn. What is it?"

Fawn held out the stack of books she carried. Another quaint Honeybee initiation ritual: the old members could command the pledges to carry their books wherever and whenever they pleased. Judging from the pile in Fawn's arms, I strongly suspected that she had emptied her locker just for the occasion. There was such a thing as misuse of power, I thought resentfully.

"Okay, Fawn," I said without enthusiasm. "Where to?"

"The library."

"The *library*? That's in the other building! I'll be late for class!"

"What a shame!" Fawn said sadly. "But Honeybees *do* have to be willing to make a few sacrifices, you know."

It would be useless to tell Fawn that I'd already collected three late slips in one day, thanks to Sonya's dawdling and the other Honeybees' "air raids." There was nothing I could do but take the books and do as Fawn commanded. Maybe if I hurried, I could get back to biology before the late bell rang. I tightened my grip on the books and hurried down the hall.

"Penny!" Fawn called behind me. "Slow down! You're walking too fast."

One thing about initiations—they sure brought out the sadist in people. I wondered if I would be like that next year, when I was a senior Honeybee, or if I would remember my own initiation and be a little more sympathetic. At last we reached the library, and I laid down the books on the table Fawn chose.

"You're a good sport, Penny," Fawn said. "I'll remember you when we take the final vote."

Yeah. Just like I'd remember her when I collected my fourth late slip from the principal's office. I crossed the short walkway connecting the two buildings and reached the biology building just as the late bell rang. I broke into a run and rounded the corner, only to be stopped again, this time by the hall monitor.

"No running in the hall," he said, and wrote down my name on the list to be turned in to the principal.

"But Adam, it's not my fault!" I insisted. "You know about Honeybee initiations, and Fawn made me carry her books, and—"

"Hey, I'm sorry, Penny. I'm just doing my job, okay?"

"But Adam, *please*!"

"Is there a problem here?" a deep voice asked.

I turned and beheld a knight in shining armor. Well, maybe not really, but that was how Brandon Phillips looked to me at that moment, tall and lean, with his black hair gleaming underneath the hall lights.

"It's nothing, really," Adam said. "Just a routine—"

"Routine, my foot!" I objected. "I've been late for class ever since I got here this morning, thanks to the Honeybees, and when I try to get to class on time for once, RoboCop stops me from running in the hall!"

"I told you, I'm just doing my job," Adam insisted. "Do you think it's easy, sitting out here and reporting your friends?"

"You're one of the Honeybee pledges, aren't you?" Brandon asked, ignoring Adam's objections.

"Yes, I am," I said, feeling suddenly weak in the knees. "That's why I'm always late for class. It's initiation week, and—"

"Oh, I know all about Honeybee initiations," Brandon assured me. "But you can't be a Honeybee if you're expelled from school on late passes. I can take care of that for you, if you want me to."

"Could you really?"

"Sure, I could." His smile revealed his gorgeous white teeth. "I've got a little clout at this school, you know. Come on."

He didn't have to tell me twice. I gladly followed Brandon to the office, where he exchanged a few words with one of the student volunteers who worked there. We left a few minutes later, minus four late slips and one hall citation.

"Amazing," I marveled. "How did you do it?"

"I have my methods," Brandon said with a mysterious smile. "Let's just say being a star athlete has its advantages."

"Well, whatever you did, it worked. Now if only I can get through the next four days, I'll have it made."

"Adam's a good guy. He just takes his job a little too seriously," Brandon said. "If you have any more trouble, just let me know."

"Thanks." I went to biology hoping for more late slips. Who could tell? Honeybee initiations might just be the best thing that ever happened to me.

But by the time I dropped Sonya off at three-thirty, I was remembering the lunch I'd missed. Instead of going straight home, I stopped at the store, since it was closer. The bell jangled as I opened the front door, and this time Mom was there to welcome me.

"Hello, honey," she said. "How was your first day of initiations?"

"One down, four to go," I answered. "Mom, is there anything to eat around here? I'm starved."

"You might find something in the back, but don't spoil your appetite for supper."

"Don't worry! I don't think there's enough food in the world to do that."

I passed through the back door into the stockroom, and then into the smaller room that served as a combination office/lounge. There sat Woody, leaning back in his chair with his feet propped on the desk and a sandwich in his hand. For me it was love at first sight. The longing, the thrill that ran through me—it could mean only one thing.

"Peanut butter!" I said, gazing longingly at the sandwich. "You're eating *peanut butter*!"

"Yeah," Woody said, looking up as I entered the small room. "Are you hungry?"

"Starved."

"If you want to go halves, I could split it," he offered.

I was overcome with gratitude. "Oh, Woody! *Would* you?"

He would. He tore the sandwich into two pieces and handed one to me. I took a big bite and closed my eyes.

"Heavenly! I don't think I ever really appreciated peanut butter until today."

Woody cocked one eyebrow in amusement. "Don't they ever feed you at home?"

"Mmmp mmmf mmmf," I mumbled.

"Come again?"

"I missed lunch," I explained between bites. "It's part of my initiation. I have to serve as chauffeur to one of the Honeybee officers every day for a week. But she took so long to get ready that we were late for school, and it was too late to buy a lunch ticket."

"Was it worth it?"

After what had happened with Brandon? Yes, yes, a thousand times yes! "It could be a lot worse," I answered. "Some of the officers are cheerleaders, and the pledges who drive them can't leave school in the afternoon until cheerleading practice is over."

"Now that's what I like to see," Woody remarked. "A real devotion to charity."

"What do you do around here, anyway?" I asked. "I can't believe Mom and Dad pay you to sit around and eat."

"No, but I come here straight from school, so your mom lets me grab a bite first thing. I'm finished eating now, though, so I guess I'd better get to work. There's a stack of boxes out there with my name on it."

But I wasn't ready for him to go just yet. Far from being inarticulate, Woody was very easy to talk to, once you got past his reserved manner. I felt a twinge of regret at losing his companionship.

"What kind of work do you do, exactly?" I asked.

"Oh, odds and ends. I do a little stocking, a little sweeping, that sort of thing. I do some light delivery work, too, when it's needed."

"Oh."

It was funny how little I knew about Woody—he was such a big part of my parents' lives. Funny, too, that I should hate to see him go. He seemed to have the same reluctance, for he hesitated at the office door and turned back.

"Penny?"

"Yes?"

"Look, I was just thinking. Do you want to do something Saturday night? Go to a movie, maybe, or a football game?"

"I'm sorry, Woody," I said quickly. "I've already got plans."

"Oh." He dug his hands into his pockets and shuffled his feet, looking so self-conscious and embarrassed that I felt sorry for him.

"Maybe some other time," I added in the

polite but totally insincere tone that people use when they don't want to hurt somebody's feelings.

"Yeah, right," Woody agreed, accepting my comment the way it was intended.

I thought about Woody after he was gone and I was alone in the office. I could hear him in the stockroom, whistling off-key as he worked. If he had asked me during the summer, I might have said yes. But not now. Not when Brandon Phillips was almost within reach.

Chapter Three

Initiation week dragged by one day at a time. I was sometimes late and usually hungry, but I didn't mind so much anymore. It was worth it, now that Brandon had finally noticed that I was alive.

The week ended with a formal pledge banquet at the Regency, a posh local restaurant. While I had spent the last five days waiting on Honeybees, Mom had been busy making me a new dress, a velvet-and-taffeta creation in garnet red. On Friday night when I put it on, I couldn't help feeling a twinge of regret that the banquet was for members only. I would have given anything if only Brandon could have seen me in it.

But when I entered the banquet room at the Regency, my earlier confidence began to fade. Seated at the head table with the other officers was Sonya Wilcox, stunning in silver sequins. Beside her sat Fawn Bailey, equally striking in black satin and lace. I had a strong feeling that neither of their mothers had made their gowns.

Self-consciously I took my place at the table reserved for pledges, and soon dinner was served. As I picked at the roast beef on my plate, I glanced around at the other pledges. They were all younger than I. Most were sophomores, except for a couple of freshmen. All were the Beautiful People of Pressler High: the jayvee cheerleaders, the recently elected homecoming court, the freshman and sopho-more beauties. I wondered all over again why they had chosen me.

I was still pondering that mystery when Sonya Wilcox rose and called the meeting to order. After the minutes of the last meeting were read, membership chairman Julie Ferguson gave a report.

"Initiations are almost over, and so far all our pledges have passed," she announced.

There was light applause at the tables.

"Not so fast," Julie cautioned. "We're not finished yet. Now comes the biggest test of all. Each pledge will have a top-secret assignment to carry out, in order to test her loyalty to the Pressler Honeybees. Fawn, will you help me pass these out?"

Fawn and Julie gave each pledge a yellow envelope with her name on the front. There was a lot of nervous giggling as the pledges tore open the envelopes and read their assignments, but when I read mine, I found nothing to laugh about. As soon as dinner was over and the meeting broke up, I approached Sonya.

"Sonya, I have a question about my assignment."

"What is it, Penny?" she asked.

"It says I'm supposed to get a copy of the Grayson High basketball playbook."

"Right. They've got a new coach this year who's supposed to be really something. We'd like to help our guys out by giving them a little inside information on Grayson's new system."

"But—"

"For you it should be easy. Didn't your folks hire a guy from Grayson?"

Suddenly I had a mental picture of Woody on the day I'd come into the shop bursting with news about the Honeybees. He'd been sitting on the floor behind the counter eating a sandwich, and on his lap was . . .

"A blue notebook," I murmured.

"A what?"

"I've seen the book before. It's a blue notebook."

"You know what it looks like? That's great! If you already know what you're looking for, you're halfway there!"

"I don't know," I said hesitantly. I couldn't help thinking of Woody tearing his sandwich in half and saving me from certain starvation. Stealing his playbook seemed like awfully poor thanks. "It just doesn't seem right."

"Penny, last year Pressler was eliminated from the state play-offs because of a last-second shot by Grayson. The game was video-taped, and the tapes showed plainly that the buzzer went off before the shot was made, but the referees allowed it anyway. That

22

didn't seem right, either. You're our big chance for revenge! There's no way Grayson can win if we know what they're going to do before they do it. We're all counting on you— not just the Honeybees, but the whole team! The whole school, even!"

The whole team. That included Brandon Phillips. I could feel myself weakening.

"But Sonya, Woody is just my parents' stock boy," I said. "I hardly even know him!"

"There are ways to fix that, you know," Sonya pointed out. "After all, you *are* a girl, and he *is* a guy. And if he ever saw you in that dress, I'll bet you'd have him wrapped around your little finger in no time."

"Well, he did ask me out Monday," I admitted, more than a little pleased at the compliment. "But I can't just—"

Sonya was delighted. "He asked you out? Penny, that's *perfect*! I knew we were right in asking you to join!"

"But I can't go out with him just for his basketball playbook!"

"Why not? You don't have to marry the guy, you know. Just go out with him a few times, win his confidence, and then—bang!"

"But Sonya, I really don't want to get involved with anybody else right now," I confessed. "You see, there's this other guy that I like, and he's just starting to notice me now that I'm pledging the Honeybees."

"But if you don't pass initiations, you won't *be* a Honeybee," Sonya pointed out. "Think about it from that angle."

I did think about it. I tossed and turned all night long, and I honestly don't know what I would have done if events the next morning hadn't made up my mind for me. I slept late on Saturday, and by the time I wandered into the kitchen at nine-thirty, Mom and Dad were already up and dressed.

"Oh, I'm so glad you're awake," Mom said, looking up as I entered the room. "The contractor wants to take another look at the store. We're supposed to meet him at ten o'clock."

"Okay," I said. "Is there anything you need me to do around the house?"

"Just one. Woody will be dropping by to pick up his check. I've already written it out. All you have to do is give it to him."

"I thought you usually paid Woody at the store on Friday afternoon," I remarked.

24

"Usually, yes. But yesterday I was home hemming your dress," she reminded me. "We won't be gone long—maybe an hour or two."

It was fate—it had to be. What else would bring Woody Williams to my doorstep, but also get my parents out of the way just long enough for me to carry out my mission? Not that they would mind me going out with Woody—in fact, Mom adored him and would probably be ecstatic. But I had a feeling that she wouldn't approve of my motives, and I couldn't really blame her.

Sure enough, Woody stopped by at about ten-thirty. I invited him in and left him waiting in the den while I went to Dad's study to get his check. When I came back, he was standing in front of the fireplace, looking at two Polaroid snapshots propped up on the mantel. I remembered what Sonya had said last night about Woody seeing me in my new dress and felt the blood rush to my face.

"Oh, never mind those," I said quickly. "They're just some pictures Dad took of me last night before the pledge banquet. It's sort of an embarrassing habit of his."

"Pledge banquet, huh? Does that mean initiations are over and you're officially a Honey-bee?"

"Except for a few odds and ends," I said with a shrug. This was dangerous ground. "Here's your check. Oh, by the way . . ."

"Yeah?"

Take it easy, I told myself. *Don't sound too eager, or you'll blow the whole thing.* I couldn't help wondering if guys felt this uncertain when they asked a girl out. I wondered if Woody had felt like this on Monday.

"Woody, my plans for tonight fell through. I know it's short notice, but if your offer of a movie still stands—"

He just stared at me, and for a moment I was afraid he was going to tell me to make like a honeybee and buzz off. It wouldn't be entirely undeserved. But then he just smiled, brushed the hair out of his eyes, and said, "What time do you want me to pick you up?"

That afternoon Melissa rented a movie and came over to watch it on my VCR. After eating lunch at separate tables for a week, we were eager to catch up on all the Pressler High gossip. We talked about everybody else's love life, but I didn't say anything about my own. For some reason I was reluctant to tell Melissa about my date with Woody.

"It seems like ages since we've done this," Melissa said, reaching for another handful of popcorn. "In fact, it seems like ages since we've even talked to each other. I'm glad we'll be able to eat lunch together next week. The old table isn't the same without you."

"Believe me, I'll be glad to eat with you, too," I agreed, tucking my feet up on the couch. "In fact, I'll be glad just to eat in peace, without having to carry somebody's tray or go get them another napkin or extra ketchup or—"

"The phone's ringing," Melissa said, grabbing the remote control off the coffee table. "Do you want me to pause the movie?"

"You don't have to. I'll be right back."

I crossed the den and picked up the receiver. "Hello?"

The voice on the other end of the line made me turn back to Melissa and make slashing motions across my throat. Melissa aimed the remote and fired. The room grew silent.

"Hello, Brandon," I said, giving Melissa a look of pure triumph.

"Hi, Penny. Are you busy?"

"Oh, no! I wasn't doing anything important," I said. Melissa made a face at me.

"Listen, Penny, how about going to the football game with me tonight? It's the last home game, you know."

"Oh, Brandon! I'd love to . . ." I began, but then I remembered this morning's extracurricular activities. "I mean, I wish I could, but I've already got plans," I added miserably.

"Oh, that's too bad," Brandon said. "Maybe some other time, then."

"Yeah. Some other time." Now where had I heard *those* words before?

Heaving a sigh of disappointment, I replaced the receiver and turned to find Melissa standing right behind me.

"Do my ears deceive me, or did you just turn down a date with Brandon Phillips?" Melissa asked.

"I had to. I told somebody else just this morning that I'd go out with him," I said bleakly.

"Wow! You've been a Honeybee for less than a week, and suddenly you've got guys standing in line! Where do I sign up?"

"It's no big deal. It's just Woody."

"Woody from the store? Penelope Collier, why don't you *tell* me these things?"

"It's nothing serious," I insisted.

"It's serious enough that you turned down Brandon Phillips," Melissa pointed out.

"Look, Melissa, it's all top secret, so I can't explain it, but I will tell you this much: it's a part of my initiation. No more and no less."

"You mean you've got to date a guy from another school? You don't have to tell me, just nod your head yes or no."

"Will you stop it? I told you it's a secret. But how can I go out with Woody, now that Brandon is finally interested in me? I'll feel like I'm being unfaithful to him!"

"That's the wrong attitude," Melissa said firmly. "You should go out with Woody tonight and make sure Brandon finds out about it. Who knows? A little competition might be good for him."

Maybe she was right, but I couldn't be sure. At any rate, only one thing was certain. To keep Brandon's interest, I had to be a Honeybee, and to become a Honeybee, I had to date Woody. What a mess!

Chapter Four

At six-thirty on Saturday night, I sat on the edge of the living-room couch, waiting for the doorbell to ring. I didn't know why I was so nervous; after all, it was only Woody, my parents' stock boy. Besides, I didn't have to get the playbook tonight. For now I would concentrate on learning more about Woody's schedule. Did he always come straight to work from school? Did he always bring his schoolbooks to the shop, and if so, where did he leave them while he was working? Did he carry his playbook every day? All this would be done very subtly, of course, so he wouldn't suspect anything.

The doorbell rang promptly at a quarter of seven. When I opened the door, I got my first surprise of the night. I was used to seeing Woody in the dingy white apron he wore at work, but tonight he was wearing a blue Grayson letter sweater that brought out the blue of his eyes. Even the rebellious strand of sandy hair had been tamed, at least temporarily. I had never thought much about Woody's life outside the shop, but suddenly it occurred to me that there were probably more than a few girls at Grayson High who would be glad to trade places with me.

"Come on in," I said, making a quick recovery. "I'll get my jacket."

It doesn't matter what he looks like, I told myself firmly. As far as I was concerned, he was just Woody from the shop. Going to the movies with him wasn't so very different from sharing a sandwich in the stockroom.

At first that seemed to be true. Things had been a little strained at the shop since Woody had asked me out and I'd turned him down, but now, alone in his car, we quickly recaptured the same easy friendship we had enjoyed briefly in the stockroom. I decided I was glad to have it back.

But when we arrived at the movie theater, the shimmer of gold satin caught my eye. Sonya, Julie, and Fawn were all there, along with several members of the Pressler Yellow Jackets basketball team. A couple of the girls nudged their boyfriends as we passed by, and the whole group cast knowing smiles in Woody's direction.

I knew why. Thanks to his Grayson sweater, all the kids knew exactly who he was and why I was with him. I wanted to remind them that the initiation projects were supposed to be kept secret. It irritated me, the way they looked at Woody as if he were a pigeon ready for the plucking. Okay, so maybe he was; they still didn't have to look at him that way. I was relieved when the group just smiled and waved, without making any attempt to join us.

"Do you want anything to eat?" Woody asked, pausing near the snack bar.

"I don't think so," I said. "I'm not really hungry."

Woody's eyebrows rose in mock surprise, but his blue eyes twinkled. "You? Not hungry? That's a switch!"

"They don't serve peanut butter here," I

explained with a smile. Actually, seeing the gang from Pressler had ruined my appetite.

We were a few minutes early, so there were still plenty of good seats to choose from. Several other couples filed in behind us, and one boy recognized Woody and called out his name.

"Woody! How's my man?"

"Man, they'll let anybody in here, as long as they've got money," Woody joked. "Penny, this is Pete Reynolds. He's a good guy, as long as you don't believe a word he says. Pete, Penny Collier. Her folks own the store where I work."

Pete raised his eyebrows. "The boss's daughter, huh? No wonder you're always in such a hurry to get to work!"

"Penny's a junior at Pressler High," Woody added.

"You'd better watch those Yellow Jackets, Woody," Pete cautioned. "You might get stung if you're not careful."

I'm sure Pete didn't know he'd made a prophetic statement.

"I'll take my chances," Woody said, as Pete sat down. "If you ask me, I think people take this Grayson-Pressler thing a little too far," he whispered in my ear.

"I do, too," I agreed. "It's always been a big rivalry, but a lot of the kids at Pressler are really steamed about what happened last year in the play-offs."

"They have pretty good reason to be," Woody admitted. "It was before my time, but I've seen the films. We got a freebie from the referee."

I was surprised. "I know that's what all the kids at Pressler say, but I never thought I'd hear anybody from Grayson agree."

Woody shrugged. "Hey, you can't argue with it when it's right there in living color. If it's any consolation, though, Grayson got eliminated in the very next game. I guess what goes around comes around."

Okay, enough small talk. It was time to get down to business. "What about this year's team?" I asked. "Are you having any trouble learning the new system?"

"Well, it's different from anything we've played before, but in a way it's easier for me than it is for starters. They're having to unlearn everything they did last year."

35

"Do you still study your playbook at the shop?"

"I usually keep it with me to look over whenever I have a minute or two. Still, you can't really learn that stuff until you get out on the court and do it—at least I can't."

I would have pursued the subject, but at that moment the lights dimmed and a hush fell over the auditorium as the big screen lit up. Just then the door at the back of the theater opened. To my dismay the whole Pressler crowd came trooping down the aisle and sat down right behind us. As the opening credits ended and the movie began, Woody reached over and took my hand. I hoped the kids behind me didn't see that. In spite of Melissa's advice, I didn't want word of this date to get back to Brandon.

The movie was an adventure film about foreign intrigue and international espionage—it seemed appropriate somehow. Still, it had an exciting plot, and by fixing my eyes on the big screen, I was able to imagine that the boy sitting next to me was Brandon Phillips. In fact, I was so successful at this little game of make-believe that, during one particularly suspenseful part of the movie, I instinctively tightened my grip on Woody's hand. He gave my hand a little squeeze in return, which made me feel extremely uncomfortable. If only Brandon had called twenty-four hours earlier, I thought, how different this night could have been!

It wasn't until after the movie, when Woody parked his car in my driveway, that I began to wonder what would happen next. Would he kiss me good night? Should I let him? Why in the world hadn't I thought of this before?

"You seem preoccupied," Woody remarked as we slowly mounted the stairs up to the porch.

"I was just thinking. . . ."

"About what?"

"The Honeybees, mostly."

"Yeah, I noticed a group of them in the lobby. They seemed to get a kick out of seeing one of their pledges with The Enemy. Were the Honeybees responsible for messing up your plans for the weekend?"

"In a way, yes." I really didn't want to elaborate.

37

"Oh. Well, I can't really say that I'm sorry," Woody said candidly. "I had a great time tonight, Penny."

"So did I."

Actually, it wouldn't have been half bad, if it hadn't been for those Honeybees sitting right behind us, watching my every move.

Then Woody put his arms around me, and I knew the big moment had arrived. *Forgive me, Brandon,* I thought. *I'm only doing this for you.* I closed my eyes and raised my lips to meet Woody's kiss. To my surprise it was kind of nice—soft and warm and comfortable, like my favorite old sweatshirt. I was a little disappointed when Woody raised his head and drew back.

You're doing this for Brandon, I reminded myself sternly. *You're not supposed to enjoy it!*

"Will you be coming by the shop tomorrow?" Woody asked.

"Probably," I said, remembering the playbook. I would be there tomorrow and every day, until my mission was accomplished. "Yes, I'll be there."

"Good. I'll see you tomorrow, then." Woody smiled and practically skipped to his car.

Chapter Five

On Monday I ate lunch with Melissa for the first time in over a week, but it was not the peaceful meal I had hoped for. Halfway through lunch period Melissa went to ask the cafeteria ladies for extra ketchup, and as soon as she was out of earshot, I was surrounded by a swarm of eager Honeybees.

"Well?" Sonya prompted, grabbing the chair Melissa had just vacated. "How did it go?"

"Not there," I protested. "I'm saving that seat for a friend."

"We *are* your friends," Sonya asserted, sitting down at Melissa's place. The other Honeybees were quick to follow her lead, and soon every place at the table was taken. David and Shane, two of the boys who had been at the theater on Saturday night, soon dragged up chairs from the next table and joined us.

"We're all dying of curiosity!" Sonya exclaimed. "How did it go with this Grayson guy?"

"It was fine," I said, nervously twisting my napkin. "Woody is really nice."

"We don't care how nice he is," Julie Ferguson said impatiently. "Did you get the playbook?"

"No," I confessed. "I think I should have a chance this week at the shop, though. He usually brings it with him when he comes to work."

"Well, it's not much, but I guess it's a start," Sonya said, obviously disappointed. "Did you find out anything else?"

"Only that the new system is a lot different from their old one," I told her, "and that some of the starters are having trouble adjusting."

David, a starter on the Pressler basketball team, leaned forward eagerly in his seat.

"Now we're getting somewhere! Exactly what is it that they're having trouble with?"

"I don't know," I said, shrugging my shoulders. "He didn't say."

"Didn't he say *who* is having trouble adjusting?"

"He just said the starters. He didn't mention any names."

"Couldn't you have asked?" Shane put in. "A lot depends on this, you know!"

"Oh, lay off, you two," Julie said, to my relief. "They went to a movie, not a basketball clinic! These things take time, you know."

"We don't have much time to spare," Shane pointed out. "The Harpersville Invitational Tournament will be here before we know it, and that marks the beginning of basketball season."

"Yeah," David agreed, "and I'd like to have plenty of time to go over that playbook, just in case we meet Grayson in the tournament."

"When will you be seeing Woody again, Penny?" Sonya asked.

"Probably this afternoon. I usually see him every day after school."

"Perfect! Keep an eye out for that playbook, will you?"

As she spoke, Sonya rose from the table and walked away. As if on cue everyone else left with her, leaving me sitting alone.

"Penelope Collier, I don't *believe* you!"

I turned quickly, startled at the sound of Melissa's voice. "Melissa?"

"I didn't think I would be very welcome at a gathering of Honeybees, so I sat at the next table and eavesdropped. Penny, you're a *spy!*"

"Shhh! Keep it down, will you?" I hissed. "Too many people know about it already, without you telling the rest of the world!"

"But Penny, *why?*" Melissa persisted.

"I told you. It's part of my initiation."

Melissa was shocked. "Then *that's* why you went out with Woody! So you could steal his playbook!"

"I'm not going to *steal* it, exactly," I protested. "I'm just going to *borrow* it for a little while—just long enough to make a copy of it. I'll see that he gets it back, I promise."

"A lot of good it'll do him then," Melissa remarked bitterly.

"I know what you're thinking, but so much

is riding on this! Brandon, the Honeybees . . . If I can't get the playbook, I'll lose it all!"

"I still think it's wrong," Melissa said stubbornly.

"Don't make such a big deal out of it, Melissa. After all, you probably would be doing the same thing if you'd been invited to join."

"Oh, no I wouldn't! No club is that important to me."

"Famous last words!" I retorted, stung by my best friend's lack of sympathy. "You'll change your tune next year when I put you up for membership."

"Don't bother," Melissa said, gathering her lunch things and getting ready to leave. "I'm not sure I want to be part of a club that requires its members to cheat and steal!"

"Fine! Be that way!" I called after her. "They probably wouldn't have you, anyway!"

After Melissa had gone, I looked down at my half-eaten hamburger. Suddenly it seemed to taste like cardboard. I couldn't remember the last time Melissa and I had argued like that. And it was all Melissa's fault for being so self-righteous. Of course I didn't *like* the idea of stealing the playbook—especially from Woody, who was turning out to be one of the nicest guys I'd ever met. But this was an extraordinary situation, and extraordinary situations called for extraordinary actions. And if Melissa couldn't understand that, well, who needed her anyway? I sure didn't. After all, I was going to be a Honeybee; I had plenty of other friends.

But I soon discovered that Melissa wasn't the only one who disapproved of what I'd been doing lately. As I left the cafeteria, Brandon stopped me on the sidewalk.

"Hey, Penny," he said. "I've got to talk to you."

"Sure, Brandon," I said breathlessly, responding at once to the serious look in his eyes. "What is it?"

"I've been talking to David Morris. He says he saw you at the movies Saturday night with some guy from Grayson."

"That's right. What about it?"

"Aren't any of the guys at Pressler good enough for you?" He asked the question in a light, teasing tone, but still there was that look—could it be jealousy?—in his eyes. Brandon Phillips jealous? Of *Woody*? I couldn't believe it! I started to tell Brandon he had it all wrong, then remembered what Melissa had said. Maybe she was right: maybe what Brandon needed to make him really interested in me was a rival. After all, he was an athlete, a born competitor.

"Good enough for me? Maybe some of them," I said, giving him what I hoped was a flirtatious smile. "And maybe some of them are a little too slow."

His interest was caught, all right. I could tell by the way he looked at me. "Penelope Collier, is that a challenge?" he asked with a sparkle in his gorgeous brown eyes.

"Take it any way you want it," I said, throwing one last sultry glance at him over my shoulder as I started down the sidewalk in the other direction.

It worked! I could feel his eyes on me as I walked away. Now I was more determined than ever to get that playbook, and the sooner the better. The next time Brandon asked me out—and I was pretty sure he would—I wanted to be free to accept.

In that frame of mind it was disappointing to get to the shop only to find Woody nowhere in sight. While Mom waited on customers and Dad met with the contractor in his office, I slipped through the back door into the stockroom, hoping to hear Woody's off-key whistling. But there was no sound at all. I wandered up and down the aisles between the rows of tall metal shelves, but I saw no sign of him.

Then I saw *it*. On the last row of shelves, right beside the door that opened onto an alley behind the shop, was a stack of school-books. U.S. history, advanced algebra, and underneath them the blue notebook. His books were here, but where was Woody? I remembered him saying that he sometimes did delivery work. That must be it. I would probably never have a better chance. I threw a nervous glance over my shoulder, then tip-toed over to the shelf. Lifting the books slightly, I grasped the notebook and carefully slid it out from under the pile.

At that moment the door beside me flew open. I gave a startled shriek, and the blue notebook, along with all the rest of Woody's schoolbooks, came tumbling to the floor.

"Penny? What's wrong?" Woody stood in the doorway, his face filled with surprise and concern.

"You—you scared me!" I stammered. Then, remembering the incriminating evidence at my feet, I dropped quickly to my knees and clumsily stacked Woody's books. "I knocked your books down. I'm sorry—"

"It's okay. I'll get them," Woody said, dashing my hopes by picking up the blue notebook and sliding it underneath the stack. "What were you doing back here, anyway?"

"I was looking for you," I said, grasping at anything that might divert suspicion.

"Well, you found me," Woody said, giving me a grin. "What did you want me for?"

"I—I forgot. . . . I'll come back later . . ." was all I could say before I ran out of the stockroom.

Chapter Six

If Monday was bad, the rest of the week was even worse. On Tuesday I arrived at the shop to find Dad and the contractor going through the stockroom making plans for the proposed renovations. The blue notebook was lying there on the shelf, just as it had the day before, but even though I stayed at the shop till closing time, I never had a minute alone to make my move.

On Wednesday, Woody was at the shop but his playbook wasn't. I made as thorough a search as I dared, without arousing anyone's suspicions, but couldn't find it anywhere. I could only assume that he had decided to leave it at school. At any rate, another day was wasted.

On Thursday, Mom had the notion of putting me to work, since I was spending so much time at the shop lately. She led me to the big metal filing cabinet in the office, where I spent the next three hours learning to file invoices. I guess it was educational, but it didn't accomplish much in the way of espionage. I wondered if any Honeybees had ever been elected on the basis of their secretarial skills. Somehow I doubted it.

But on Friday things finally took a turn for the better. I had joined Melissa in the school cafeteria for what had become our daily argument about my Honeybee initiation when Brandon came over and pulled out a chair. Melissa and I might disagree, but like a true friend, she discreetly faded away at Brandon's approach.

"Hi, Penny," he said as he sat down beside me. "Can we talk a minute?"

I gave him my most dazzling smile. "Sure, Brandon. What's up?"

"Shane Walters told me the whole story about you and that Grayson guy. He said you're only dating him to get us a copy of the Grayson basketball playbook. Is that right?"

"Well, yes," I said hesitantly. "But it's supposed to be secret, so—"

"Oh, don't worry about that. You know how these things get around. Have you gotten it yet?"

"No," I confessed. "I was hoping to get it this week, but things are pretty hectic around the shop, now that we're getting ready to remodel."

"How long do you think it'll take?"

"Oh, a couple of months, probably," I said.

"A couple of months!" Brandon's voice was filled with alarm.

"At the very least. The building's about seventy-five years old, you know. Mom says she shudders to think what condition the wiring must be in."

To my surprise Brandon started to laugh. "Not that! I'm not talking about remodeling the store. I meant how long do you think it'll take to get the playbook?"

"I wish I knew!" I gave him a brief summary of my week's activities. "I hope things go better this afternoon. If they don't, it'll be

51

a whole week wasted. The Honeybees are going to give up on me if I don't hurry up."

"No, they won't," he assured me. "I'll see to that."

"How?" I asked.

"Like I told you—I have some influence around here." Brandon leaned closer to me. "Anyway, are you going out with that Grayson guy again this weekend?"

"It all depends. . . ."

"Depends on what?"

"Two things. Whether I can get the play-book this afternoon, and whether he asks me."

"You mean, if he asks you'll go?"

"I'll have to," I said simply. "For Pressler."

Brandon sat back in his chair, giving me a look filled with admiration. "I think that's great. You'll never know how much we appreciate all you're doing for us, Penny."

I thought it would be wonderful to be praised and admired by Brandon, but something about it irritated me a little. He made it sound as if going out with Woody was the ultimate sacrifice, when it wasn't like that at all.

"It's not so bad, really," I said.

"Still, we can't have you getting too chummy with these Grayson guys. After all, you'll soon be a Honeybee, and Honeybees belong with Yellow Jackets." He rose and collected his lunch things, then touched my cheek, making me shiver. "Get that playbook, Penny. Get it soon."

Unfortunately, it was not to be. When I arrived at the shop that afternoon, I discovered that Mom had big plans for me, and they didn't include snooping through the stockroom. Instead she put me to work emptying the shelves in the showroom so they could be moved. If only it had been the stockroom instead! It would have been the perfect opportunity.

"We'll be going to the bank to sign the papers next week," Mom explained, "and after that the construction will start. Things will be awfully crowded for a while, so we'll have to make the best use of the space we've got. If shopping here is too inconvenient, our customers might decide to go somewhere else."

With Mom directing, Dad and Woody rearranged the shelves on the showroom floor.

Since she changed her mind several times during the proceedings, it turned out to be a complicated and lengthy task. Fortunately, a customer came in to order business stationery, and Mom was forced to abandon her role of supervisor long enough to go to the office and get the books of sample letterhead styles.

"Okay, that'll do," Dad said to Woody and me, giving us a sly wink. "Quick, you two, see if you can get those shelves restocked before she comes back!"

"Mom is absolutely obsessed with this remodeling thing," I told Woody as we worked together. "She seems to be convinced that the building is going to burn down around us if we don't modernize it immediately."

"Well, she's right in a way," Woody admitted. "There's no telling how old the wiring is. Besides, just think of all the other things that could go wrong—the plumbing, the gas lines, the—"

I laughed. "Okay, okay! So the place is a death trap, and we're all doomed!"

"I don't think anybody ever died from leaky plumbing," Woody said with a grin. "Still, I guess it's time something was done about the place. Your dad showed me the plans just the other day. I probably won't even recognize the store by the time I get back."

Startled, I said, "Oh, are you going somewhere?"

"Hadn't you heard? This is my last day."

I had been stacking reams of copier paper onto a shelf, but at that piece of unwelcome news, two packs slipped through my arms and fell to the floor, hitting me on the foot.

"Ouch!" I yelped.

"Hey, be careful," Woody said, a bit too late. "Are you okay?"

"I'll live," I said, gingerly rubbing the toe of my shoe. "I didn't need that foot, anyway. You just—surprised me. I didn't know you were leaving."

"Well, I'm not *leaving*, exactly. But basketball practice starts next week, so my hours will have to be cut way back."

"I thought you'd been having basketball practice all along," I said.

"During PE, yeah. But beginning Monday we'll be practicing till five o'clock, or even later. I'll only be able to work on Saturdays."

Terrific! The one day I *didn't* go to the shop was the only day Woody would be there. It

55

was bad, but it could have been a lot worse. Woody had really given me a scare for a minute. Still, I knew I had to make the best use of the time I had left. I stacked the last ream of paper onto the shelf and stepped back to admire my handiwork.

"Well, if this is your last day, we ought to do something special," I said brightly. "You know, to celebrate."

Woody grinned and raked his sandy hair out of his eyes. "To tell you the truth, we're playing a scrimmage game tomorrow night. Coach Andrews wants a chance to see how we do in a game situation. If you don't think you'd be too bored—"

I thought fast. I might not get the playbook this week, but here was a chance to do something almost as good. I would be able to scout the Grayson team in person. Of course, what I didn't know about basketball would fill a dozen playbooks, but I was sure Brandon could give me some tips on what to look for. At any rate, it was too good an opportunity to pass up.

"I'd love to go," I told Woody. "And I promise, I won't be bored at all."

Chapter Seven

I spent Friday evening and all day Saturday preparing for Woody's scrimmage game, but it wasn't the kind of preparation normally associated with dating. On Friday after I left the store I went to the library and checked out half a dozen totally incomprehensible books on basketball. I read until late into the night and hit the books again on Saturday morning, but it was clearly hopeless.

"Now I see why Woody said you can't learn this stuff from a book," I muttered aloud, rubbing my bleary eyes.

Exhausted, I looked up Brandon's father's name in the phone book and dialed his number. Normally I would have let Brandon make the first move, but as I said earlier, this was definitely *not* a normal situation. I heard the phone ring once, twice, and then Brandon's deep, thrilling voice came through the line.

"Hello?"

I swallowed hard and said, "Hello, Brandon. This is Penny Collier."

"Penny!" He sounded pleased, even elated, to hear from me. "What's up? Did you get the playbook?"

"No, not yet. But I did get an invitation to watch the Grayson Bulldogs scrimmage tonight."

"Hey, that's great! You should be able to get all kinds of information!"

"Well, there's only one problem," I said, embarrassed to make such a confession to Pressler's reigning basketball star. "I—uh, I don't know very much about basketball. I thought maybe you could tell me some things to watch for."

"Sure," Brandon said at once. "Got a pencil?"

"Just a minute." I scurried to find a pencil, thinking how strange it was that they were never around when you needed them. At last I found one in a kitchen drawer full of odds and ends. I grabbed it and a pad of paper and returned to the telephone.

"Okay," I said. "Fire when ready."

"First of all, be sure to notice what kind of defense they run. Last year they ran a man-to-man, but they have a new coach this year, so they may have switched to a zone."

"Man-to-man or zone," I echoed, obediently writing it down. "How will I know which is which?"

"Oh, boy," Brandon said with a sigh. "This is going to be tougher than I thought. Maybe you could just ask the guy after the game. You know, tell him how wonderful he was and ask a lot of questions."

I could tell by Brandon's tone of voice that I had let him down. "Is there anything else I should look for?" I asked, eager to make it up to him.

"Well, they lost several of last year's starters to graduation, so there will be a lot of new guys on the team this year. You could notice if there's anybody in particular that we ought to watch for. That shouldn't be too hard." I had the depressing feeling that Brandon thought he was dealing with an imbecile. "And notice where most of the shots are coming from—whether they're from outside, or underneath the basket. Think you can handle that?"

"I'll do my best."

We said good-bye, and I returned to my basketball books to try to learn the difference between a zone and a man-to-man defense.

By the time the doorbell rang at six-thirty, I had basketball running out my ears. Zones, traps, presses, screens—it was like a foreign language.

I opened the door and invited Woody in. He was wearing his blue-and-gray warm-ups, and I noticed all over again how well his school colors matched his eyes. We chatted with Mom and Dad for a few minutes, then Woody led the way out to his car and opened the passenger door for me. On the seat lay a gray gym bag with the Grayson High Bulldogs logo printed in blue.

"Here, let me get my stuff out of the way," Woody said. "That way you'll have a little more room."

He ducked into the car and tossed the bag onto the backseat. It hit a stack of schoolbooks, causing them to slide across the seat. I caught my breath in an audible gasp.

Underneath the books lay the familiar blue notebook.

"What's the matter?" Woody asked.

"Your—your algebra book," I said, making a quick recovery. "It's just like the ones we use at Pressler."

"That's interesting," Woody said, giving me a grin. "If you get too bored during the game, you can always start on my homework."

"I don't think you'd want me to," I said, sliding onto the seat. "I don't know much more about algebra than I do about basketball!"

Woody went around the car and climbed in on the driver's side. "Well, let me give you a crash course. There's this ball, see, and this basket, and the object of the game is to make the ball go through the basket. That's why they call it basketball."

"I'm not quite as bad as that!" I protested, giggling. It was weird, in a way—I didn't mind being teased by Woody, but if Brandon had said something like that, I probably would have been embarrassed to death.

It was still early when we arrived at Grayson High. When we got out of the car, I was careful to leave my door unlocked. I was determined to come back later for the play-book. This was the best chance I'd had yet, and I didn't intend to blow it.

I noticed that the crowd was still thin—mostly the players and their families. Some of the guys, like Woody, had brought a date. He took my hand as we walked from the parking lot to the gym. Several of the others glanced in our direction, and I knew I was being sized up as Woody's girlfriend. Once we were inside the gym, Woody led me to the bleachers on the opposite side of the building.

"The starters are the home team, so you'll be sitting on the visitors' side," he explained. "Unless you want to sit in the home stands and cheer for Pete instead."

It took me a minute to remember that Pete was Woody's friend who we'd run into at the movies. "Oh, is Pete a starter?" I asked.

"I'll say he is! In fact, he's the reason I'm *not* one."

"You sub for *Pete*?"

"Is that so surprising?" Woody asked, giving me a curious smile.

"Just unexpected, that's all. When we saw him in the theater, you two seemed like such good friends."

Woody laughed at that. "Am I supposed to hate him just because he's a better player than I am? We go at each other pretty hard in practice, don't get me wrong. I like to think I make him work for that starting position, at least a little bit. He'll be graduating this year, so I'll get my chance next year, but I'll miss him. In a weird way we make each other better. Does that sound strange?"

Actually, it did. I tried to imagine Brandon having that kind of a friendship with someone who beat him out of a starting position, and failed. Oh, well. Brandon was just more competitive than Woody, that was all.

Woody took my arm as we climbed the bleachers to the fifth row. We both sat down, but after a couple of minutes Woody stood up and picked up his gym bag.

"I'd better get to the locker room before they send out a search party," he said reluctantly. "I hate to abandon you here, though. I'd introduce you to Pete's sister Sharon, but she's on the other side."

"I'll be fine," I assured him. "I'm sure I'll find something to keep me busy until game time."

As soon as Woody was out of sight, I left the bleachers and hurried back the way we had come in. The parking lot was beginning to fill up, and I had to look around for a minute before I spotted Woody's blue Honda. As I reached the Honda and opened the door on the passenger side, I felt as if everybody from Grayson High was staring at me. *It's no big deal,* I told myself firmly. *To them, you're just Woody's date, getting something out of Woody's car.*

My heart beat wildly as I reached into the backseat, picked up the blue notebook, and flipped a few pages. Sure enough, it was full of diagrams showing a basketball court littered with Xs and arrows. I couldn't make heads or tails of it, but I was sure that Brandon and the rest of the Yellow Jackets could. I shut the door with a snap and stuffed the book into my purse, thankful that I had decided to bring the big leather shoulder bag I'd bought a few weeks ago.

There! I'd done it! I pushed the playbook down to the bottom of my bag, then rearranged the contents to completely cover it up. Satisfied, I slammed the car door shut, being sure to lock it this time, and headed back to the gym.

I made it with only seconds to spare. No sooner had I resumed my place on the bleachers than the locker door flew open and Woody's team ran onto the court to begin their warm-up drills. I breathed a sigh of relief and settled down, instinctively drawing my purse closer to me.

I had intended to watch the game with an open mind, keeping a sharp eye for the things Brandon had mentioned, but I discovered that it wasn't easy to remain objective. I knew Woody was fighting for a starting position, and I couldn't help hoping he would get it, in spite of the fact that he was hopelessly outclassed by his best friend.

Not that Woody was bad; in fact, he looked pretty good to me. At one point he and Pete were battling for a rebound near the visitors' stands, and I got a good look at him. His face was flushed with exertion, and his eyes blazed with intensity, their color a brilliant blue against the pink of his face. I found myself revising my earlier opinion of his lack of competitive spirit. And when he blocked one of Pete's shots late in the second quarter, I leapt to my feet and cheered, completely forgetting my real reason for being there.

Although the game was exciting, nobody was really surprised when the starters beat the second string 58–56. Still, I took an irrational pride in the fact that seven of those fifty-six points belonged to Woody. When the final buzzer sounded, he returned to the bench just long enough to grab a towel and give his face a quick wipe.

"I'm off to shower and change," he called to me. "Be back in a minute!"

I nodded to show that I'd heard him and settled back down to wait. True to his word, Woody came back a few minutes later. His hair was wet from showering, and he'd exchanged his sweat-soaked jersey and shorts for blue jeans and a yellow sweater.

"Pete wants to know if we want to meet him and Sharon at the Pizza Spin," he said, offering a hand to steady me as I came down the bleachers to join him. "Is that okay with you?"

Was it okay? Unexpected, maybe, but not unwelcome. In fact, I figured I might be able to pick up more basketball strategy by listening to Woody and Pete discuss the game than I could ever have gotten out of Woody alone.

"It sounds fine," I answered.

Woody and I reached the Pizza Spin ahead of Pete and his sister, so we chose a booth for the four of us. I slid into the red vinyl seat, and Woody sat down beside me.

"Well, Penny, what did you think of the game?" he asked.

"I think the Pressler Yellow Jackets have got their work cut out for them. What kind of defense do you call that?" I asked, remembering Brandon's advice.

"I'd call it a pretty weak one, myself," Woody said with a dry laugh. "Which one do you mean? We started off in a 1–2–2 zone and switched to a box and one in the second half."

"I didn't see anybody in a box," I said, totally confused.

"Not that kind of box," Woody said, grinning down at me. "Here, I'll show you."

He took a paper napkin from the metal holder and quickly sketched one end of a basketball court, adding Xs to represent the

67

players. As he explained, I leaned closer to get a better look. I couldn't help noticing how good he smelled—not a heavy cologne smell, just fresh and clean. I wondered what Brandon smelled like, and if I would ever get close enough to him to find out.

"A box and one is a special defense that combines a zone and a man-to-man," Woody was saying. "These guys"—he pointed his pencil at four Xs arranged in a square—"play zone, while this other guy plays man-to-man against the other team's best player. Only in our case it didn't work very well."

"I thought you did just fine," I told him, though I still didn't quite understand what he was talking about.

Woody was quick to downplay his role in the game, but I could tell he was pleased. "I made a couple of good plays on defense, but my free-throw shooting was lousy."

"I didn't think it was that bad."

"Well, I did," a third voice put in. "Anybody who misses four out of five free throws ought to be shot!"

"If you could shoot a basketball half as well as you shoot off your mouth, you'd be in the

NBA by now," Woody joked as Pete sat down on the seat opposite us. "I really missed those shots on purpose, Penny. I didn't want to hurt Pete's feelings by beating him out of his starting spot."

"Very funny," Pete said with a grin.

A petite blond girl slid into the seat next to Pete. "I think you did just great, Woody."

"Well, I'm glad to see that *somebody* around here appreciates me," Woody said. "Penny, this is Sharon Reynolds, Pete's younger sister. Sharon, Penny Collier. She's a junior at Pressler."

"But we'll let her eat with us anyway," Pete said generously. "What kind of pizza should we get?"

We agreed on pepperoni and mushrooms, and Woody and Pete went to place the order.

"I didn't know Woody had a girlfriend," Sharon remarked. "How long have you two been dating?"

"Well, I'm not his girlfriend, exactly," I hedged. "Woody has worked for my parents since June, but we've only recently gotten to know each other."

"Woody is really a special guy," Sharon said

softly, then quickly added, "My brother Pete thinks the world of him, though you'd never guess it to hear them talk."

My eyes widened as a thought suddenly struck me. Was Sharon Reynolds in love with Woody?

Chapter Eight

I kept on glancing at Sharon as we ate, and by the time we had munched our way through a large pepperoni-and-mushroom pizza, I was sure I was right—Sharon *was* in love with Woody! Not that she threw herself at him or anything like that. There was just a certain softness in her voice when she spoke his name, a certain light in her eyes when she looked at him. It was the same way Mom and Dad sometimes looked at each other, and the same way—good grief! It was the same way Woody looked at me!

Looking back, I wondered how I could have missed realizing how he felt about me. I had been more than willing to go out with Woody so I could get my hands on his playbook, but I hadn't thought much about why he had asked me out in the first place. I guess I'd been so caught up in worrying about the Honeybees that I had become blind to everything else.

I didn't have much to say during the drive home because I was thinking about my latest discovery. Woody was one of the nicest guys I knew, and he had no idea that he was being used by a girl he cared about. Until tonight I hadn't really thought this playbook stunt would hurt anybody.

"You're awfully quiet tonight, Penny," Woody remarked as he parked the car in my driveway. "What's on your mind?"

"I was just—thinking," I answered evasively. "Mom and Dad will really miss you at the shop next week."

"Just Mom and Dad?"

"No, not just Mom and Dad," I said with a little smile. "I'll miss you, too."

"I'm not gone forever, you know. I'll be back after basketball season is over. It sure was nice of your folks to let me work Saturdays, instead of letting me go and hiring somebody else."

"They would never do that, Woody," I told him. "They think too much of you."

"I think a lot of them, too. After all, they hired me with no work experience whatsoever."

"I think it paid off for them."

Woody grinned at me. "Hey, I'm the real winner here. If I hadn't gone to work for them, I never would have met you." And with that he leaned over to give me a light kiss on the cheek.

I felt just awful. Woody should be dating a nice girl like Sharon, who obviously worshiped the ground he walked on. He deserved so much better than this! Feeling a sudden rush of tenderness for him, I wrapped my arms around his neck and returned his kiss with a lot more enthusiasm than I had shown on our first date. Encouraged by my response, Woody tightened his arms around me and kissed me in a way that was not at all soft or cozy or comfortable. That kiss made me forget all about the playbook, the Honeybees—even Brandon Phillips. By the time we finally drew apart, we were both breathless, and I could feel my heart pounding wildly inside my chest.

What is happening to me! I thought as I got out of the car and hurried up the stairs and into the house.

"Mom! Dad! I'm home," I called once I was inside. It was funny, my voice didn't even sound like my own.

"We're in the den, honey, if you'd like to join us," Mom answered.

As I started in the direction of the den, I caught a glimpse of myself in the mirror that hung in the foyer. My eyes were wide and dilated, and my lipstick was all smeared. No doubt about it—I looked like a girl who had just been thoroughly kissed.

Now look here, I told my reflection firmly, *you've got to snap out of it. You had a job to do, and you did it. You were supposed to get the playbook from Woody Williams, and you got it. So what if he happened to kiss you in a way that sent shivers down your spine? That's got nothing to do with anything.*

"Coming, Mom," I said, and after I had

repaired the damage to my makeup, I went to join my parents in the den.

"This is perfect," Sonya said at lunch on Monday, turning the pages reverently. "Just perfect."

"Tell us how you did it, Penny," Julie said.

All around the cafeteria table the Honeybees and Yellow Jackets leaned forward eagerly, unwilling to miss a single word. Brandon was at my side, his dark eyes aglow with admiration.

"It was nothing, really," I insisted, smiling shyly at Brandon. "Be careful with it, Sonya. I'll make a copy of it this afternoon and see that the original gets back to him."

"Fine," Sonya said. "In the meantime I'll order your jacket. Congratulations, Penny! You're officially a Honeybee!"

"What about the game, Penny?" Brandon asked. "How did Grayson look?"

"They looked pretty good to me, but Woody didn't agree. He scored seven points, but he was pretty disappointed with his free-throw shooting. He only made one out of five."

"Did you remember any of the things I told you to watch for?" Brandon persisted.

"Well, I did ask about their defense. They started off in a zone, and then they switched to one in a box," I reported proudly.

"I think she means a box and one," Brandon said, grinning across the table at David and Shane. "What kind of a zone did they start with? A 2–1–2?"

"That was it. No, wait a minute," I added thoughtfully. "It was a 1–2–2—or did Woody say 2–2–1? Or 1–2–3, maybe—"

Brandon laughed. "There's no such thing as a 1–2–3. Unless you've got six men on the court instead of five! Forget it, Penny. Just copy the playbook. That should tell us everything we need to know."

I offered him an apologetic smile, well aware that I had let him down again. How was it that I had felt so wonderful just a minute ago, and now I felt so stupid?

It was a relief when the subject of the playbook was dropped and the conversation shifted to gossip. After butchering the reputations of half the students at Pressler, Sonya and the other Honeybees rose to leave, followed by David, Shane, and the other guys. But Brandon lingered at my side after the others had gone.

"Well, congratulations, Penny," he said. "Looks like you made it."

"Yeah, it sure looks that way," I agreed. Just being alone with him made my heart pound so loudly that I was sure he could hear it.

"So now that you're a Honeybee, how about going to the preseason tournament with me this weekend? The first round starts Friday night, you know."

I was so overjoyed I could hardly speak. "Friday night sounds fine," I managed.

"Great! I'll pick you up at six."

Wow! I'd been a Honeybee for less than fifteen minutes, and already my dreams were beginning to come true!

"Guess what?" I announced when I saw Melissa in biology. "I'm in! I passed my initiation with flying colors, and I'm in!"

"Congratulations, I guess," Melissa said doubtfully. "Pardon me for not dancing in the streets."

"Oh, come on! You know how much this means to me," I pleaded. "Besides, if you're going to act that way about it, I won't tell you who I've got a date with this weekend!"

"Woody again?"

"No, *not* Woody again!" I said triumphantly. "I'm going to the tournament with Brandon!"

Melissa gasped. "You're kidding!"

"Would I joke about a thing like this? He asked me last period, during—" I broke off, seeing Melissa's expression of astonishment fade into a worried frown. "What is it, Melissa? What's wrong now?"

"I was just wondering. What are you going to do if Woody asks you to go with him?"

"What else? I'll tell him the truth," I said firmly, squashing the tiny seed of doubt that Melissa had planted in my mind.

Melissa stared at me. "Penny! You'd tell him you only went out with him for his *playbook*?"

"No! Not *that* truth! The *other* truth—that I already have a date with somebody else."

"I can't believe you're just dumping Woody like that!" Melissa muttered.

"And *I* can't believe *you're* making such a big deal about nothing! I told you all along that I wasn't serious about Woody, and I haven't done anything to give him the impression that I was—at least, I haven't done very much," I amended feebly, remembering that last kiss.

Still, Melissa was not convinced, and I was relieved when the late bell rang, sparing me any more of her scolding. For the next hour I studiously ignored her while Mr. Mason delivered a long and monotonous lecture on the mating habits of the black-widow spider.

"After the mating process is complete," Mr. Mason concluded, "the female destroys her partner—hence the name 'black widow.' Are there any questions?"

"You mean the female just uses the male and bumps him off when she's through with him?" Lisa, one of the other girls in the class, asked.

"Precisely," said Mr. Mason, obviously pleased that his lecture had impressed someone.

Lisa shuddered. "I think that's awful!"

"It may sound barbaric to us humans," he agreed, "but it's perfectly natural to the black widow."

"Black widow?" Melissa muttered behind my back. "Sounds more like a Honeybee to me!"

Chapter Nine

When the final bell rang, I left school and headed for the shop, eager to tie up the few loose ends that remained of my Honeybee initiation. In spite of what I had told Melissa, I felt really bad about stealing Woody's playbook, and I wanted to return it to him as soon as possible. I would use the copier at the store and make a photocopy to give to the Honeybees tomorrow. As for the original, I planned to leave it in the stockroom for Woody to find on Saturday. With any luck he would think he'd left it there last week.

I had almost convinced myself that returning the playbook kind of canceled out my "borrowing" it in the first place. By the time I reached the store, I was glad to see that things were pretty busy, for a Monday. Mom was occupied with several customers, while Dad was shut up in his office calculating last month's sales taxes.

"Penny, honey, I'm glad you stopped by," Mom said. "Tomorrow at three-thirty your father and I have an appointment to meet with the loan officer and the contractor to sign the papers, so we'll need you to watch the store for a couple of hours. Mrs. Godwin will be in her shop next door, in case you have any trouble."

"Sure, I don't mind. Mom, do you mind if I use the copier? I'll only be a minute."

"Is it for a school project?" she asked.

"Yes, in a way. It's for the Honeybees."

"How many copies do you need?"

"One complete set. It's about a dozen pages."

Mom raised her eyebrows. "A dozen! Well, all right, just this once. But remember, we have to buy that paper, you know, and it doesn't come cheap."

"Thanks, Mom. I'll be done in a minute."

I crossed the room to the copier, eager to get started before Mom could think of any more questions. Luckily the new shelving layout blocked her view of the copier, giving me complete privacy. I couldn't help thinking of how hard Woody had worked to arrange everything to Mom's satisfaction, and it made me feel guilty all over again.

Twenty-four hours later the Yellow Jackets had their playbook, and I had my Honeybee jacket. I wore it the rest of the day, and when school was over, I went straight to the shop to model it for Mom and Dad.

"Ta-da!" I sang as I threw open the door, setting the bell jangling.

"Oh, Penny, you're just in time," Mom said, hurrying to the office to get her purse. "Business has been slow today, so you shouldn't have much trouble. Remember Mrs. Godwin is next door at the shoe store, in case you need anything. I left her telephone number beside the phone."

"We'd better get a move on, Helen," Dad put in. "We don't want to be late."

"Mom, I got my Honeybee jacket today," I pointed out, following her from the showroom to the office and back again. "Isn't it great?"

"What? Oh, yes, it's lovely, dear. We've got

to go now, but you can show it to us tonight. Remember to call Mrs. Godwin if you need help. Her number is—"

"Right beside the telephone," I finished for her. "Got it."

After they were gone, the store seemed quiet and lonely. I couldn't really blame Mom and Dad for not being more excited about my jacket; after all, this remodeling project had been a dream of theirs for a long time, just like joining the Honeybees had been a dream of mine. Still, it was sort of a letdown. I left the showroom and went to the rest room in the rear of the store, confident that the bell would warn me if a customer came in. The mirror over the bathroom sink was spotted and cracked, but it was good enough for me.

I turned this way and that, admiring the way the gold satin shone in the light. I traced my finger along my name, embroidered in black on the left side of the jacket. ("ynneP," it read in the mirror.) I turned my back to the mirror and craned my neck around to see the black-and-gold honeybee appliquéd on the back.

Everything I had dreamed of had come true. I should have been ecstatic, but instead

I felt depressed. Although I was a full-fledged Honeybee and had the jacket to prove it, I really didn't feel any different inside. I even had a date with Brandon Phillips, but I still didn't feel beautiful and popular like Sonya and Fawn and Julie and the others.

I yawned deeply. Maybe I was just tired. Last night I had been so excited about my date with Brandon that I hadn't slept very well. I'd try to catch up on my sleep tonight. . . .

The sound of the telephone ringing out front snapped me out of it. Probably Mrs. Godwin, I thought, calling from the shoe store to check up on me. I switched off the bathroom light and ran to answer the phone. Although the office extension was closer, I took the call in the showroom, just in case any customers came in. I slid behind the counter, picked up the receiver, and lifted it to my ear.

"Good afternoon. Collier's Office Supply."

"Penny?" said a familiar voice. "This is Woody. Listen, have you seen my playbook around the store anywhere? I could have sworn I had it with me on Saturday night, but I can't find it anywhere."

I swallowed hard. "Uh—hang on a second. I'll look." I lowered the receiver and covered the mouthpiece with my hand. I waited a minute, then uncovered it. "Yes, it's here in the stockroom," I said. At least that was true.

"Whew! I couldn't figure out what in the world I had done with it! Thanks, Penny, I'll be over in a little while to pick it up."

At the prospect of seeing Woody, my spirits felt unaccountably lighter as I returned the receiver to its cradle. Maybe that was why it had seemed so quiet in here—it was because Woody wasn't here, whistling cheerfully as he worked. *Now if only I could wake up*, I thought, slapping myself lightly on the cheek. I wished Woody would hurry, or a customer would come in—anything to give me something to do. I just couldn't seem to stay awake.

I got my wish a few minutes later, when a woman came in to buy a box of typewriter ribbons. I pulled out the big reference book from under the counter to look up the right model number, and as I flipped the pages, the woman's nose twitched.

"What is that strange smell?" she asked.

I sniffed but didn't smell a thing.

"We're remodeling," I answered vaguely. After all, Mom said the customer was always right. Besides, next week the place would probably smell like sawdust and paint and all the other things normally associated with building.

I located the correct typewriter ribbon and rang up the sale. The customer paid me in cash, and soon I was alone in the shop once more, with nothing to do but wait for Woody. I ran a hand wearily across my forehead. My eyelids suddenly seemed so heavy, I could hardly keep them open. *Maybe if I could rest for just a minute, I'd feel better,* I thought. I sat down on a high stool and folded my arms on the counter, laying my head on top of them. The bell would wake me if anybody came in, I reasoned. Besides, it would only be for a minute. . . .

The next thing I knew, someone was shaking me violently by the shoulder.

"Penny! Penny, wake up!" a guy's voice was saying urgently. The voice was familiar, but I was too sleepy to try to identify it.

"Go 'way," I mumbled, shaking my head irritably.

"Penny, listen to me! You've got to get out

of here! Can you walk?" A pair of strong hands dragged me to my feet, but my knees buckled, and I slid to the floor. "No, I guess not," the voice said with a dry laugh.

What happened next is sort of fuzzy. I was vaguely aware of being lifted in someone's arms and carried out the door. Over my head I could hear his voice saying something about a gas leak and an ambulance, and suddenly I seemed to be surrounded by people.

"Oxygen!" someone yelled, as something was strapped across my nose and mouth. "We need oxygen over here!"

This is just great, some remote, still-functioning part of my brain whispered. *You finally got a date with Brandon Phillips, and now you're going to be too dead to enjoy it!*

Chapter Ten

When I woke up, I was lying on a bed in a small, sparsely furnished room. The walls, the sheets on the bed—everything around me was white. No, not quite everything. In one corner of the room an angel in blue jeans and high-top sneakers sat reading a sports magazine.

"Am I dead yet?" I asked in a voice that was little more than a whisper.

At that the angel looked up and smiled. "No, I think you're going to be around for a while," he said, laying aside his magazine. Getting up from his chair, he crossed the tiny room and sat down on the edge of the bed.

"Oh, Woody," I said, blinking dazedly at him. "It's you! Where am I?" Discovering that I was fully dressed, I threw off the covers and sat up in bed.

"Be careful," Woody warned, putting a steadying arm around me. "You may be light-headed for a little while."

He was right. As soon as I sat upright, my head started swimming. It felt good to lean against Woody's shoulder for support.

"Where am I?" I asked again.

"You're at Parkway Medical Center. There was a gas leak at the store."

"Mom and Dad . . . ?"

"Are on their way. Mrs. Godwin called the bank and told them what happened. They ought to be getting here about any minute now."

The door opened a crack, and we both turned, expecting to see my parents. Instead it was the emergency-room nurse who appeared in the doorway.

"Are you awake, honey? I thought I heard voices in here," she said. "You're a very lucky young lady, you know. If your boyfriend had come along fifteen minutes later, it might have been too late."

"My boyfriend?" I echoed.

"I hope you don't mind," Woody murmured apologetically as the nurse bustled around the room. "They asked me if I was a relative. That was the best I could do on short notice."

The nurse looked surprised. "You mean he's *not* your boyfriend? Honey, if I were you, I'd grab him up before some other girl beat me to him!"

Woody was obviously embarrassed—his face turned bright red. I thought it was rather sweet. Fortunately for both of us, there was a light tap on the door at that moment, and Mom and Dad entered the room.

"Penny! Darling!" Mom flew to my bedside, alternately fussing over my health and praising Woody's heroism. "I knew something like this would happen if we didn't do something about that old building! I just *knew* it!"

"Now, Helen, there's no need to get all excited," Dad said, giving me a hug and a kiss. "The doctor says Penny will be just fine, and something's going to be done about 'that old building' starting tomorrow. Now if you'll help Penny get ready to leave, I'll go down to the business office and see how much it's going to cost me to get her out of here." Dad gave me a quick wink, then turned and followed the nurse out of the room.

"Well, now that your folks are here, I guess I'd better be getting on home," Woody said, rising from his seat on the edge of the bed. He went as far as the door, then paused and turned back. "Oh, by the way," he said, his blue eyes dancing with mischief, "whatever you did, I forgive you."

My heart skipped a beat. "What do you mean?"

"I was hoping maybe *you* could tell *me*. I rode with you in the ambulance, and all the way to the hospital you kept telling me how sorry you were."

"I—I did?" I asked breathlessly, gripping the sheet until my knuckles turned white. "What about?"

"You never did say. You only said you were sorry, that you didn't want to do it, but you had to because they made you. Mean anything to you?"

I shook my head. "Not a thing," I mumbled.

* * *

Although the doctor said that I was fully recovered, Mom wasn't convinced. She was determined to keep me home from school the next day, even though I insisted that I felt fine. It was probably just as well that she won out in the end, because when I saw the next morning's newspaper, I felt distinctly unwell. There on the front page was a complete account of the rescue under the thrilling headline, "Local Teen Saves Boss's Daughter!"

"Oh, no!" I moaned.

"What's wrong, honey?" Mom asked, probably afraid that I was suffering a relapse.

"Have you seen today's paper?"

She smiled. "Yes, I have. Wasn't that a nice article about you and Woody?"

"*Nice?* Mom this is totally embarrassing! I'll be ashamed to show my face at school tomorrow!"

Still, I eagerly turned the page to finish reading the article. Woody had said very little to me about his own role in the incident, and it wasn't until I read it in the paper that I got the full account of what had happened. Even then I noticed that the newspaper report relied heavily on quotes from Mrs. Godwin and the paramedics who had taken the call. It wasn't hard to guess why: Woody was naturally reserved, and I couldn't imagine him opening up easily for a newspaper interview, even (or maybe especially) when he was the hero.

According to the paper Woody had come into the store to get his basketball playbook, which he had left there a few days earlier. The minute he came into the shop, he detected an unusual odor and recognized the smell as natural gas. He discovered me semi-conscious behind the counter, and finding that I couldn't be roused, he had picked me up and carried me bodily from the building. He had then taken me next door to Godwin's Shoe Town, where he had phoned for help. When pressed, he admitted that he still didn't have the playbook he had gone after in the first place, "but," said the newspaper, "the modest hero replied, 'It just didn't seem that important anymore.' "

I felt like scum.

When I returned to school on Thursday, I found Melissa waiting for me in the parking lot. Two weeks ago that wouldn't have seemed unusual, but things had changed between Melissa and me over the last few days.

"Hey, Penny," she said, hurrying over to me as I locked my car doors. "Can we talk a minute?"

"Sure," I said, surprised at her serious tone. "What's up?"

" 'What's up?' I read in the newspaper that my best friend nearly gets herself killed, and all she has to say for herself is, 'What's up?' Honestly, Penny, you could have called, you know!"

I had to smile a little at her vehemence. "To tell you the truth, I almost did."

"So what stopped you?"

"I was afraid you might tell me I got exactly what I deserved."

"Penny!" Melissa cried, insulted. "You're my best friend, remember? Okay, so maybe I'm not absolutely wild about what you've been doing lately. So what? Besides, maybe you were right. Maybe I was just jealous because you were invited to join the Honeybees and I wasn't."

"No, Melissa," I said quietly, "*you* were right. About Woody, I mean. I felt funny about it before, but now, after this . . ." I let the sentence trail off unfinished. "Do you know what I mean?"

"Yeah, I think so," Melissa answered, and I had the feeling that she did.

Once we reached the main building, I discovered that everything was just as I had feared. It seemed that every student, teacher, and administrator at Pressler High had seen the newspaper, and though the reactions were varied, they all agreed that it was the most exciting thing that had happened around Pressler in a long time. Several of the girls thought the whole thing sounded terribly romantic and wanted to know all about my rescuer. The Honeybees seemed to think the situation was hilariously funny—as if I had deliberately gassed myself as part of my plan to entrap Woody! Brandon grumbled about all the media hype, and I suspected that he was a little bit envious of all the attention Woody was getting.

All in all, the only person who *didn't* seem to want to talk about the episode was the hero himself. I halfway expected Woody to call, but by Friday night I still hadn't heard from him. I told myself that I was glad, that it was better this way. After all, from now on I'd be dating Brandon, and how do you dump the guy who just saved your life? Still, it hurt my pride to think that Woody could rescue me one day and forget all about me the next.

Chapter Eleven

That night I prepared for my date with Brandon with mixed feelings. I selected my clothes with extra care in an effort to recapture the excitement I had felt earlier in the week when he had first asked me out. After trying on and discarding several different combinations, I finally settled on a pair of black jeans acid washed to a pale gray, and a bright yellow sweater with a black tick-tack-toe design on the front. Besides being Pressler's school colors, the outfit would look great with my black-and-gold Honeybee jacket.

When I'd finished getting dressed and doing

my hair and makeup, I was satisfied with my appearance, but not with my emotions. That excited feeling seemed to be gone for good, and I didn't know why. I had dreamed of this night for so long, but now everything was all wrong. I wasn't even sure exactly when the change in me had taken place, but it seemed to have begun somewhere around the time I woke up in that hospital room to find Woody sitting at my bedside.

"Well, don't you look pretty," Mom remarked as I joined her and Dad in the den to wait for Brandon. "Where did you say you and Woody were going?"

"To the basketball tournament at Harpersville High School. Only I'm not going with Woody; I'm going with Brandon Phillips."

Mom nodded. "Oh, yes, I remember you telling me now. I guess I just forgot during all the excitement this week."

"Look, Mom," I said irritably, "Woody is a nice guy and all that, and I appreciate what he did for me, but does that mean I can't go out with anybody else?"

At my outburst Mom and Dad both turned to stare at me in surprise. I realized that I had overreacted.

"I'm sorry," I said, feeling more than a little bit foolish. "I guess I'm just nervous. I've liked Brandon for an awfully long time, and now that I'm actually going out with him— well, I'm just antsy, that's all."

The doorbell rang soon afterwards, and I invited Brandon in and introduced him to Mom and Dad. He said all the right things, and Mom and Dad were both pleasant to him, even commenting on how well my new Honeybee jacket matched his Pressler letter sweater. Still, I couldn't quite shake the feeling that they were comparing him unfavorably to Woody.

At last we said our good-byes, and Brandon led me outside to where his sleek black sports car waited in the driveway. Its windows were heavily tinted, and when I got into the passenger seat and Brandon shut the door behind me, I felt suddenly trapped. At long last I was alone with Brandon Phillips. What now? What was I supposed to say to him? We barely even knew each other. What could we possibly talk about on the twenty-minute drive to Harpersville?

"Well, who do you think will win tonight?" Brandon asked, climbing into the driver's seat beside me.

"Pressler, of course," I said brightly, swallowing my nervousness.

"I think you're probably right," Brandon said matter-of-factly. "Harpersville wasn't all that strong last year, and they lost four of their starting five. It should be a pretty easy win."

"But it's their tournament," I pointed out. "They have the home-court advantage."

Brandon dismissed this with a snort. "If you ask me, 'home-court advantage' is a bunch of baloney. Nine times out of ten the best team will win no matter where the game is played."

I slid down lower in the seat. Why was it that whenever I tried to discuss basketball with Brandon, I ended up sticking my foot in my mouth? For the rest of the drive I let him do the talking. He told me all about Pressler's strengths (which were many) and weaknesses (which were few), and I made suitably admiring or sympathetic noises. Maybe I didn't come across as being particularly intelligent, but at least I managed to avoid making a fool of myself.

When we reached Harpersville High, the gym was already beginning to fill up. I wasn't really surprised, since four schools were represented in the tournament. Grayson would meet Lee High School in the first game, and afterwards Pressler would play Harpersville in the late game. Then tonight's winners would play each other tomorrow night for the championship.

Each side of the gym had been divided in two, giving each school its own section of bleachers. Pressler's section was easy to spot, since a group of Honeybees and their dates sat near the top of the stands. The girls' satin jackets and the boys' letter sweaters blended into a black-and-gold mass that was easily recognizable even from a distance. Taking my hand, Brandon led the way through the crowds to the Pressler stands.

David and Fawn moved over to make a place for us to sit, and soon after we were settled in our seats, the Grayson and Lee teams ran out onto the court to begin their warm-up drills. I leaned forward to look for Woody among the Grayson players warming up at the far end of the gym. I soon found him, a tall, slim figure in his familiar blue-and-gray sweats. Seeing him again, even from this distance, made me realize just how much I had missed him over the last few days, and how disappointed I was that he hadn't called.

"Hey, Penny, which one do we have to thank for the playbook?" Brandon asked, following my gaze to the opposite end of the court.

I hesitated a moment, reluctant to bring his name into the conversation. "Woody," I said at last. "Woody Williams."

"Which one is he?"

Since Woody's warm-up suit covered the number on his jersey, it was difficult to single him out. "There he is," I said after a minute or two. "He's got the ball right now."

"The one who just missed his lay-up?"

I winced as Woody's shot hit the rim and bounced off. "That's him," I said.

"He must be a forward," Brandon remarked.

"How did you know?" I asked in surprise.

"His height," Brandon answered. "My guess is that he's, oh, six one, maybe six two. Too short to play center, but taller than most guards. Is he a starter?"

"No. Second string."

Brandon nodded, and I had the feeling he

was pleased about that. Soon Woody and the other subs returned to the bench, while the five starters took their positions for the opening tip-off.

"All right, Grayson," Brandon said, leaning forward to watch, "let's see you win this thing!"

I turned to him in surprise. "You mean you *want* Grayson to win?" I'd had the impression that he wanted to see Grayson lose.

"Sure, I do! I want them to win tonight so we can beat them to a pulp in the championship tomorrow."

Brandon got his wish. By the time he, David, and the other Yellow Jackets left at the end of the third quarter to suit up, Grayson had established a fifteen-point lead, and they never let go of it. As for my own school, Pressler jumped out in front early, thanks to Brandon's outside shooting, and we easily defeated the Harpersville Cougars. Brandon was elated. After the game we went to the Pizza Spin, and all the way into town he talked about nothing else but how great it would be to avenge last year's loss.

"Looks like everybody else had the same

idea," Brandon remarked, searching for a space in the restaurant's crowded parking lot.

Sure enough, the Spin was jammed with players and fans from all four schools. As Brandon pushed his way through the crowd to the counter and placed our order, I looked for a vacant booth. I finally spotted one in a secluded corner of the dining room and sat down to reserve it. All around me I could hear kids talking excitedly about tomorrow night's championship game, but I couldn't share their excitement. I was secretly glad that Woody's team had won tonight, and of course I was glad to see Pressler beat Harpersville. Still, I had hoped that Pressler and Grayson wouldn't meet each other, at least not for a while. Lost in thought, I didn't realize that I had company until someone spoke my name.

"Hi, Penny."

"Woody!" At the sight of him standing beside my table, my heart gave a little leap— whether from a guilty conscience or something else, I wasn't sure. "I saw you," I said. "I thought you did great."

"Yeah, listen to you! I never got off the

bench all evening!" Woody replied ruefully, sliding into the red vinyl seat opposite me.

"That's what I mean—you did great at keeping it nice and warm," I joked, and Woody laughed.

"So how are things at the shop?" he asked, propping his elbows on the table and resting his chin in his hands. His hair was hanging down in his eyes as usual, and I suppressed a sudden urge to reach across the table and brush it back.

"Well, Dad says they got the leak repaired. To tell you the truth, I haven't been back since Tuesday."

"It ought to be perfectly safe now," Woody assured me. "Still, I can't blame you for wanting to stay away."

Had I been avoiding the shop over the last three days? Maybe so, but not for the reason Woody thought. "I'm not afraid to go back," I said. "It's just that—well, it seems too quiet around there, now that you're gone. I sort of miss hearing you whistle off-key while you work in the stockroom."

Woody sat back in his seat, arching his eyebrows in mock indignation. "What do you mean? I do not whistle off-key!"

I giggled. "You do, too! You can't carry a tune in a bucket!"

"Okay, so maybe I can't," Woody admitted with a grin. Then his smile faded, and his tone grew serious. "You look great, Penny. You're fully recovered now, right?"

I nodded. "The doctor says so." But gazing into Woody's eyes, I began to wonder. I felt suddenly dizzy. Maybe I was suffering a relapse. I quickly looked down at the red-and-white-checked tablecloth and began to play nervously with the salt shaker. "Woody, I don't think I've ever thanked you . . ." I began.

"Now don't start that," Woody said firmly, reaching across the table to take my hand in his. "You don't have to thank me, Penny. It's thanks enough just to—"

"Ahem!"

Brandon stood there beside the table, pointedly clearing his throat. Woody looked up at Brandon, then back at me, comprehension dawning in his blue eyes.

"Oh! Hey, I'm sorry! I didn't know—I thought you were—" He looked so embarrassed that I thought his face was going to melt all over the table.

"It's okay, Woody," I said softly, giving his hand a quick squeeze before he pulled it away and stumbled awkwardly out of the booth.

"I'll say one thing for you, Penny," Brandon remarked as he watched Woody cross the crowded dining room. "When you do a job, you don't do it halfway."

"What do you mean?"

Brandon chuckled. "I mean you've not only gotten his playbook, you've also turned the guy into a blithering idiot. The guy's totally nutzoid over you. I *love* it!"

I hated it when Brandon or the Honeybees talked about Woody like that. "Brandon, he saved my life!" I reminded him angrily.

"How could I forget? His name was all over the front page of the paper." He chuckled again. "I'd love to see the big hero's face when he finds out he's really a big patsy."

"He's not going to find out," I said emphatically. *"Ever."*

"Yeah, I guess you're right. Still, it's a shame to have to keep such a good joke to ourselves." But I wasn't laughing, and Brandon eyed me intently across the table. "Penny, you've done a great job. This isn't the time to start getting sentimental about it. Look at it this way—you didn't do anything to him personally. I mean, after all, he doesn't even play."

I clung to that thought as I tried to choke down the pizza slices that a waitress delivered to our table. Brandon was right, I told myself. Woody was little more than a bench warmer; he admitted that himself. The purloined playbook wouldn't really affect him at all.

Sipping my soda, I scanned the dining room for a glimpse of Woody. The crowd was thinner now, and I spotted the back of his sandy head at a table about halfway across the room. As I watched, Sharon Reynolds rose from the table and crossed the room. She stopped at the jukebox, pumped a couple of quarters into the slot, and made her selections. The music began to play as she returned to Woody's table and sat down close to him.

Something about the sight of them together made my stomach twist itself into a hard knot, though I knew I should be happy. Everything was working out perfectly. Woody deserved a girl who would be crazy about him, and Sharon definitely was. She was sweet, too, and pretty—though I strongly suspected that she wasn't a natural blond.

Stop it! I told myself firmly. *You have absolutely no right to be jealous. You can't have it both ways.* Woody had served his purpose, and now he had Sharon, and I had Brandon. After all, that was what I wanted, wasn't it?

Chapter Twelve

I had begun my date with Brandon feeling that something was wrong, and by the time he took me home, I was sure of it. I hardly said a word during the twenty-minute drive, but Brandon was so busy analyzing his performance in the basketball game that he didn't seem to notice or care. It was weird— I had never realized how self-absorbed he was until tonight. I leaned back against the leather upholstery and let Brandon's monologue roll over me in waves, relieved that I didn't have to think of anything to say.

At last we reached my house, and together we got out of the car and mounted the steps to the front porch. My heart should have been racing at the prospect of being kissed by Brandon, but it wasn't. Instead I just wanted to get it over with and put an end to this evening as soon as possible.

"How about tomorrow night?" Brandon asked as we reached the front door. "Same time, same place?"

"No, I don't think so," I answered.

He stared at me as if I had suddenly sprouted two heads. "What? You can't miss the big game tomorrow night!" he protested. "Especially when you did so much to help us win."

He had a point there. I had started this mess, and no matter how badly I wanted to forget the whole thing, I had to go back tomorrow night to see it through.

"Oh, I'll be there, all right. It's just that— well, I promised a friend I would go with her," I said, hoping I could count on Melissa to back me up.

"Too bad," Brandon murmured, drawing me into his arms. "We belong together—the Yellow Jacket and his Honeybee."

Then he pressed his lips to mine. I had

always imagined there would be bells and fireworks when we finally kissed, but there was nothing—no bells, no fireworks, nothing at all—only a sense of letdown, like the way you feel on Christmas morning when all the presents have been opened and the thing you wanted most isn't there.

"You're sure you won't change your mind about tomorrow night?" Brandon asked huskily, coming up for air.

"Positive," I assured him as I gently slipped out of his arms.

"Well, then, I guess I'll see you in my dreams," he said, giving me a wink before he turned and headed back to his car.

"Yeah—in my dreams," I whispered sadly, as I watched him drive away. Corny, maybe, but true. Brandon had been my dream guy, but now I was wide awake.

"All right, Penny," Melissa said on Saturday afternoon, curling up cross-legged on my bed. "Tell me all about it! How was your big date with Brandon?"

How could I tell Melissa that for me the high point of the evening had come when

Pete Reynolds sat down between Woody and Sharon, making me realize that they were a threesome instead of a couple?

"It was okay," I said, forcing a smile.

"Is that all? Just 'okay'?" Melissa asked, obviously surprised. "After all you did to land him?"

"Okay, okay! It was great!" I said, struggling to work up a little enthusiasm. "Brandon scored twenty-two points, and we won the game."

"Tell me something I don't already know, for heaven's sake! Is he a great kisser?"

I hesitated a moment over that one. "I guess, but—"

"But what?"

"I don't know. Maybe he was *too* good. I had the feeling that I was only the latest in a long line of girls."

"You've got to be realistic, Penny," Melissa pointed out. "Brandon's almost eighteen years old, and he's awfully popular. You can't expect to be the first girl he's ever kissed."

"No, that's not what I mean. It was almost like he was more interested in showing off his technique than he was in me personally."

I couldn't help thinking of the last time

Woody had kissed me. Maybe he lacked Brandon's skill, but he more than made up for it in sincerity.

"Remember, it was only your first date with Brandon," Melissa continued. "Maybe your expectations were a little too high. The next one will be better, just wait and see."

"There won't be a next one," I said bluntly.

"You don't think he'll ask you out again?"

"He already did. I turned him down."

"Penny!" Melissa gasped. "I thought you were so crazy about him! What happened?"

"Well, after the game last night we went to the Pizza Spin, and Woody was there, and Brandon said such mean things about him—" I buried my face in my hands and burst into tears.

"Penny, are you in love with Woody?"

"Yes—no—I don't know! All I know is that I betrayed Woody so I could join the Honeybees and impress Brandon, and now I wish I'd never heard of any of them!"

"Gosh, Penny, I'm sorry. I had no idea!"

I sniffed. "Well, go ahead. Here's your chance to say 'I told you so.' "

"Penelope Collier! You know me better than that!" Melissa scolded.

I tried to smile. "Yeah, I guess I do. You're a really good friend, Melissa. By the way, I told Brandon that I was going to the game with you tonight. I hope that's okay with you."

"Gee, Penny," Melissa said guiltily, "ordinarily it would be fine. But last night I met this neat guy from Harpersville, and—but I can always cancel. After all, I can't let my best friend down."

I shook my head. "Don't you dare cancel your date! You go and have a terrific time."

"You're sure you don't mind?" she asked uncertainly.

"Positive," I said with a lot more confidence than I felt. "I'll find someone else to go with. And who knows? Grayson just might win. Woody said that their new system was pretty complicated. How could the Yellow Jackets learn in four days what the Bulldogs had been working on for weeks?"

I worked so hard at convincing myself that Grayson could win that when I took my place among the Honeybees that night, I was feeling pretty optimistic.

Unfortunately, the feeling didn't last long. For the first few minutes of play, the two teams seemed to be evenly matched. But as the first quarter progressed, Pressler had the advantage of seeing Grayson run the very plays that the Yellow Jackets had studied all week. Throughout the second quarter the Yellow Jackets were able to anticipate the Bulldogs' every move, and gradually Pressler began to build a sizable lead. The Honeybees and the other Pressler fans were cheering like mad, and I even heard one boy say that the only thing keeping Grayson in the game was Pete's lethal outside shot.

And then, with five minutes left in the first half, Pete fell into the bleachers trying to retrieve a loose ball. One of his teammates offered a hand to help him to his feet, but when Pete stood up, he leaned heavily against the other boy's shoulder. The referee called an official's time-out, and Pete limped to the bench, favoring his right leg. There were a few seconds of confusion on the Grayson side-lines, and a moment later Woody stripped off his warm-ups and entered the game.

I watched him take his place on the court with a strange mixture of pride and misery— pride that Woody was finally getting a chance to play, and misery because I could no longer kid myself that the stolen playbook wouldn't really matter. I don't think I had ever believed it, anyway. But now the most important thing to me was not who won the game, but that Woody might be hurt by what I had done. I realized to my dismay that Melissa's suspicions were right. As if this situation needed any more complications, I had fallen in love with Woody Williams.

It wasn't a good night for Woody, and it didn't help to know that it was all my fault. Grayson struggled to work the ball inside for a close shot, but since Pressler knew all their plays in advance, it was useless. Shane blocked Woody's first shot, and on his very next trip down the court, Brandon stole a pass from him. Pressler's lead climbed to ten points, but Woody finally got his chance to score when Brandon fouled him as he brought in a rebound.

"Sink it, Woody!" Grayson's cheerleaders shouted as the two teams lined up for the free throws.

Woody bounced the ball on the floor a couple of times, then took aim and fired. I held my breath as the ball rolled around the rim for what seemed an eternity. Then I suppressed a groan when it fell harmlessly to the floor. Woody's second shot was no better. The ball hit the front of the rim and bounced off, right into Brandon's hands. I forced myself to cheer along with the other Honeybees, but my heart ached for Woody. He looked thoroughly disgusted with himself as he ran to the other end of the court.

Woody's missing those free throws apparently made him a target for the Yellow Jackets. It seemed as if he were being fouled every time he touched the ball, and his free-throw shooting didn't improve much with practice. Then, with only a few seconds remaining in the half, Woody made a fast break for the basket. As he went up for the shot, Brandon charged into him, slamming him against the wall.

I was on my feet in an instant. "He did that on purpose!" I shouted.

"Shhh! Sit down!" Fawn hissed, grabbing me by the arm and jerking me back down.

"But Brandon did it on purpose!" I repeated.

"Of course he did it on purpose!" she said

impatiently. "Why should he let Grayson have an easy lay-up? Especially when that guy is a lousy free-throw shooter."

"He is not!" I cried, coming to Woody's defense. "He's just having a bad night, that's all."

"I don't know what you're so hot about," Fawn said. "You're the one who said he was lousy in the first place. Didn't she, Sonya?"

"That's right," Sonya agreed. "Don't you remember, Penny? It was that day in the cafeteria, after you watched Grayson scrimmage. You said he only connected on one out of five."

Suddenly I felt both hot and cold at the same time. I thought I was going to be sick. "But—but I didn't mean—"

"I guess when he came into the game, Brandon must have remembered what you said and decided to make the most of it," Sonya concluded.

My mind was in such turmoil that I didn't even see Woody attempt his next two shots. The Yellow Jackets were out to get him, and it was all because of me. All because of one stupid, thoughtless remark I'd made to impress a bunch of people that I didn't even like, now that I'd gotten to know them. At that moment the buzzer sounded, ending the half. And suddenly I knew what I had to do.

Chapter Thirteen

As usual halftime brought a mass exodus of people from the bleachers onto the floor on their way to the concession stand or the rest rooms, but somehow I managed to push and shove my way through the crowd. I caught up with Woody just outside the locker-room door.

"Woody!" I cried, grabbing his arm to get his attention. "I've got to talk to you."

He looked down at me in surprise. "Penny? What's up?" In spite of the disaster on the basketball court, he seemed pleased to see me. I only hoped he would still feel that way after he'd heard what I had to say.

"I know what's wrong out there—why Grayson is having such a hard time," I told him. "The Yellow Jackets have a copy of the Bulldogs' playbook. They've been studying it all week!"

Woody's forehead creased in a thoughtful frown, and a droplet of perspiration rolled down the side of his face. He swiped at it absently with the towel that hung around his neck. "Well, that sure would explain a lot of things that have been going on out there," he admitted. "But still, I don't get it. How would they get hold of a copy? I can't believe that anybody on our team would—"

"Believe me, it's true," I interrupted.

"How do you know?"

"Because I . . ." I hesitated for a moment. It was so tempting to make up something, tell him anything except the truth. But I knew I had to be honest with Woody. After the rotten way I had treated him, I owed him that much. "Because I did it," I said miserably.

Woody took a staggering step backwards, as if I'd punched him in the stomach. "You *what*?"

126

"I did it. I got it out of your car the night of the scrimmage game. I had to take it—it was part of my Honeybee initiation. Please try to understand, Woody, I—"

"Oh, I understand, all right! I understand a lot of things now!" Woody's blue eyes blazed with an anger all the more frightening because it was so out of character. "There's a pretty decent stereo in my car, you know. Why didn't you take that, too, while you were at it? Or maybe I should have counted my hubcaps after I took you home!"

"I'm not a thief!" I cried.

"No, you're worse than a thief, because you let me think that you . . ." He broke off, swallowed hard, then went on. "I'll bet you and your hotshot boyfriend had a great time laughing at me while I made a first-class fool of myself!"

Woody's face blurred as my eyes filled with tears. When I spoke, my voice was little more than a whisper. "I never laughed at you, Woody."

"No, I bet you didn't. You were probably too embarrassed!" he said grimly. "It must have been pretty humiliating for a Pressler Honeybee to be seen in public with her dad's hired hand—especially when he's just second string for Grayson."

"But Woody, I—"

At that moment the locker-room door flew open. "Williams, if you want to play in the second half, you'd better get your butt in here!" Grayson's coach shouted, and Woody strode away from me.

"But Woody, I love you!" I called after him.

He had already reached the locker-room door, but at that he turned back, and the reproachful look in his eyes cut me to the heart.

"If that's your idea of love, I'm better off without it," he said quietly, and disappeared into the locker room, slamming the door behind him.

Blinded by tears, I turned and stumbled back the way I had come. I couldn't stay there another minute. All I wanted to do was get my things and go home. I found my place in the bleachers and shrugged on the gold satin jacket I had once been so proud of, remembering the day I had discovered the Honeybees' invitation in my locker. If I had known then how it all would end, I would have thrown the yellow envelope into the trash without even opening it!

"Hey, Penny, where are you going?" Sonya asked.

"Home," I muttered.

"Oh, but you can't miss the slaughter," Fawn protested. "Not when you did so much to bring it about!"

"Penny, you look like you've been crying," Sonya remarked, peering intently at me. "What's wrong?"

"I just had a fight with Woody."

"Woody?" Fawn repeated. "You mean the guy you took the playbook from?" Her eyes widened. "He doesn't know, does he?"

"He didn't, but he does now," I answered. "I told him everything. I had to. I just couldn't live with myself anymore, knowing that I'd done him so dirty."

Fawn gasped. "I can't *believe* you'd do that to the Honeybees, after all we've done for you! We only invited you to join because you had a better chance at getting a Bulldog playbook than anybody else. And now you've spoiled everything, all for some Grayson bench warmer!"

My chin went up defiantly. "If you ask me,

that 'Grayson bench warmer' is worth ten of any Honeybee I've ever met!"

"I suppose you know we could have you blackballed for this," Sonya spoke up.

"I'll save you the trouble," I said as I stripped off my gold jacket and threw it onto her lap. Then I grabbed my purse and made my way down the bleachers without a backward glance.

I headed for the nearest exit, but before I got there, the doors of both locker rooms flew open, and the two teams ran out onto the court to begin the second half. Woody passed by so close to me that I could have reached out and touched him if I'd dared, but he showed no sign of having seen me at all. I knew I should leave. I *wanted* to leave, but I couldn't seem to force my stubborn feet to move. So I watched the entire second half from where I stood, alone and unnoticed at the end of the bleachers.

And what a half it was! Woody played like a man possessed. I've never seen anything like it. Grayson began to cut into Pressler's lead. It was obvious that the Bulldogs had made some changes during halftime, though

I didn't understand enough about basketball to know exactly what those changes were.

In spite of Grayson's scoring in the second half, time was still on Pressler's side. Grayson still trailed by one point as the final seconds ticked down. Woody put up a desperate last-second shot, but the ball bounced off the rim as the buzzer sounded, and the Pressler stands went wild.

But that wasn't the end of it. A referee blew his whistle and waved his arms wildly. There was pandemonium in the gym as the referees met with the coaches on the sidelines. A moment later an announcement came over the PA: the Grayson player had been fouled in the act of shooting, and though the clock had expired, the game would not be officially over until after the two free-throw attempts.

Once again I held my breath as Woody stepped up to the line. He took the ball from the referee, bounced it a couple of times, then shot. It swished through the net without even brushing the rim—the game was tied. The noise in the gym was deafening as Woody attempted his second shot. This time the ball spun provocatively around the rim for what seemed like hours but was really only a few seconds. Then the entire Grayson team rushed onto the court as the ball dropped in.

Woody was surrounded by his teammates, and I quickly lost sight of him. I turned and made my way to the nearest exit. The cold wind stung my cheeks as I pushed the door open, the cheers of Grayson's fans ringing in my ears. Obeying a sudden impulse, I turned back for one last look. The entire Grayson team had gathered on the court for the net-cutting ceremony following the champion-ship game. I could see Woody clearly now—he'd been boosted up onto the shoulders of some of his teammates and was hacking away at the net with a pocketknife. Maybe it was my imagination, but I couldn't help thinking that for someone who'd just helped his team win the championship, he didn't look very happy.

I stayed up past midnight that night, hop-ing and praying that Woody would call, if only to yell at me, but of course he didn't. After all, what more could he have to say to me than he'd already said? At last I gave up and went to bed, but not to sleep. I tossed and turned for most of the night, wondering what to do, and by the time morning finally came, my mind was made up.

I'm not in the habit of throwing myself at boys, but I knew Woody wouldn't approach me again—not after the way I'd hurt him. It was up to me to make the next move, and even though it was risky, I loved Woody too much to give him up without at least trying to make amends.

I dressed quickly and ate a hurried breakfast, offering Mom a vague excuse for going to town, then hopped into my little car and headed straight for the shop.

The bell rang as I pulled the door open, and Mrs. Carter, the retiree who ran the shop on Saturdays, looked up from her perch behind the counter.

"Hello, Penny," she said as I came inside. "What brings you here on a Saturday?"

Suddenly I wasn't so sure this was a good idea. But I couldn't back out now. "I, uh, came to see Woody."

"He's in the back," she said, nodding toward the stockroom.

"Thanks."

I crossed the room to the door and timidly pushed it open. There was Woody, in his familiar white apron, sweeping the stockroom floor. Since he had his back turned, he hadn't seen me come in. I hesitated for a moment, then took a deep, quivering breath and tapped lightly on the open door.

"I'll be done here in just a—" Woody broke off abruptly as he turned and saw me standing in the doorway. "Oh. It's you."

His reaction wasn't exactly encouraging, but I was determined to carry out my plan.

"Can I come in?" I asked hesitantly.

Woody shrugged. "Hey, your folks own the place."

"Woody, I wanted to talk to you about— about last night."

He started sweeping again. "Yeah, what about it?"

"You played a great game last night," I said sincerely. "Congratulations."

"I did okay," he said. A faint ghost of a smile flickered across his face, then disappeared. "In a way I guess I owe it all to you."

That surprised me. "To me?"

"As long as I was mad enough to stay focused on the game, I didn't have to think

134

about you, about how you—" Woody began to sweep with such vigor that I thought he would wear a hole in the floor.

"Oh, Woody, I'm so sorry," I whispered.

"You don't have anything to be sorry for, Penny. You wanted to be a Honeybee. You did what you had to do, that's all, and like a jerk I believed what I wanted to believe." Woody paused for a moment and put his broom aside. "I don't remember exactly what I said to you last night, but I'm sure it was pretty rotten. I'm sorry about that."

Trying very hard not to cry, I said, "You didn't say anything that I didn't deserve. And—and I don't blame you for hating me."

Woody sighed. "But I *don't* hate you. Oh, I tried, I'll grant you that," he added with a short, humorless laugh. "But it was no use. That's what makes it so bad. I should have been smart enough to guess that something was up when you agreed to go out with me, but I wasn't. And you know what? If I had it all to do again, I'd probably do the same thing. If it's anybody's fault, it's mine, for being so gullible."

"If it makes you feel any better, you're not the only one," I said. "I was so thrilled at being invited to join the Honeybees, but the only reason they wanted *me* was because I had easy access to *you*."

Woody began to smile—a *real* smile this time. "I never knew I was so important," he said, taking me by the hand and drawing me close to him. "Well, here we are—a pair of jerks. Sounds like we deserve each other."

"Oh, Woody!" I cried, wrapping my arms around his neck. "I was afraid I'd lost you for good!"

"No way! You're not going to get rid of me that easily," he said, tightening his arms around me.

"But I still feel bad about the playbook. I wish there was some way I could make it up to you."

"Forget it, Penny," he said gently. "Maybe it was all for the best, considering the way things turned out. After the game last night, Coach Andrews told me he liked the way I played in the second half so much that he's going to let me start Tuesday night when we open our regular season against Harpersville."

"That's great! But you mean Pete still won't be able to play?" I asked.

Woody grinned. "Oh, Pete will be fine by

Tuesday. But a basketball team needs *two* forwards, you know."

"No, I didn't," I confessed, but my ignorance didn't seem to bother him in the least.

"Anyway, unless you're sick of basketball for obvious reasons, I sure would like to have you there to see my first varsity start."

"I can't think of anything I'd rather do," I said contentedly, snuggling closer to him.

"I can think of something *I'd* rather do," Woody said, and bent to kiss me gently on the lips.

Then he kissed me again, and his kisses were so sweet—sweeter than honey.